$\int$ Bartlett AND
THE $Ice\ Voyage$

First published in Australia in 1998
Allen & Unwin, Sydney, Australia

First published in Great Britain in 1999
Bloomsbury Publishing Plc, 38 Soho Square, London, W1V 5DF

Copyright © Text Odo Hirsch 1998
Copyright © Text illustrations Andrew McLean 1998
Copyright © Cover illustrations Giles Greenfield 1999

ISBN 0 7475 4614 2

Printed in Great Britain by Clays Ltd, St Ives plc

10 9 8 7 6 5 4 3 2

ABOUT THE AUTHOR

Odo Hirsch was born in Australia where he studied medicine and worked as a doctor. He now lives in London. He writes novels for adults and children. His first children's book, *Antonio S and the Mystery of Theodore Guzman*, was shortlisted for the 1998 Children's Book Council of Australia Award for Younger Readers.

Bartlett and the Ice Voyage

Odo Hirsch

Illustrations by Andrew McLean

BLOOMSBURY

Chapter 1

IN THE PAST, it was not unusual for a king or queen to rule more than one country. Four was usually the maximum. It is difficult to rule more than four countries, and perhaps not altogether wise. But once there was a Queen who ruled *seven*. Her father, the King, died when she was only nine, and left four countries of his own. When she was twelve she inherited two more lands from a great-aunt whom she had never even met. And finally one of her generals thought it would be nice to give a special gift for her sixteenth birthday—so he conquered an extra country just for the occasion.

The Queen, of course, had been taught from her earliest years that she must love each of her countries as if she had no other. But the only one she had seen was the one in which she had been born. In those days, there was no really quick way of travelling around. There were no aeroplanes, cars or trains. The fastest way to get from place to place was in a carriage drawn by horses. The only way to cross the sea was in a sailing ship blown by the wind. People rode camels in the deserts and took elephants into the jungles, climbed mountains on mules and crossed ice in sleds pulled by husky dogs. And if they had no horses or camels or elephants or mules or dogs—they walked.

The Queen's seven lands had *everything*. There was snow in the north and desert in the south, mountains in the middle and vast blue oceans between one country and the next. The Queen could not possibly have crossed all these obstacles. It would have taken far too long, and she would have had no time left for anything else. A Queen who has to look after her Court is much too busy for that.

But this didn't mean that the young Queen knew nothing about the lands that belonged to her. On the contrary, she knew a great deal. It was her duty to know, and it was also a pleasure.

There were always travellers and explorers who had come back from one place or another. The most fascinating explorer of all was Mr Sutton Pufrock, who had been everywhere when he was younger. He was old now, of course, and rarely got out of bed, yet he was never without a faraway story to tell, just as if he were a traveller still. The Queen often asked for him to be brought to the palace so she could hear him speak, and her footmen would fetch him on a stretcher. Sutton Pufrock always had a stubble on his chin, for he rarely shaved, and his forehead was broad and high. He waved his walking-stick wildly when he got to the exciting parts of his stories, and those who strayed too close were

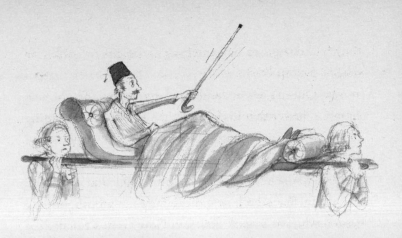

sometimes hit on the head.

Yet travellers often exaggerate, as the Queen knew, and Sutton Pufrock, with his whirling walking-stick, probably exaggerated more than anybody else. No, the only things you could really trust were those that you saw with your own eyes. Every year, the people in the Queen's countries sent special presents for her birthday. The Queen could see *these* for herself. As soon as she had unpacked the presents for one birthday, she began to look forward to the next. For a month in advance she was too excited to concentrate on anything else.

There was hardly a thing that could be moved, carried or dragged that had not been sent to the Queen as a present. Since no two of her countries were alike, no two presents were the same. And it wasn't only furniture, ornaments, chess-sets and woven carpets that the Queen received. Crates arrived containing unusual animals that no one at Court had ever seen before, with strange names written on labels hanging around their necks.

The first to arrive was a giraffe. He came as a present for the Queen's coronation, and being only nine, she was barely able to reach his knee. The Queen was too young to choose where to put him, so the Prime Minister and the Stablekeeper had to decide for her. It was no simple matter. There was nowhere with a roof that was high enough! They kept him in his crate for a month, hoping that the giraffe's neck had somehow been stretched by his difficult sea journey, and that it might shrink with time. Every day the Stablekeeper took him out for a walk through the town on a leather leash. But it wasn't long before they realised that the giraffe, who was obviously quite young, was actually growing. Eventually they let him loose in the park that surrounded the palace. Soon he was a familiar sight, cantering with his loose, loping run or standing with his head lost in the trees. People walking outside the palace wall sometimes looked up to find his soft, curious eyes gazing down at them.

After the giraffe, a rhinoceros turned up. There was nowhere for him either, so they put him in the park as well. Visiting ambassadors got a terrible fright when they were out for a stroll and the rhinoceros suddenly appeared in front of them. His horn was two feet long! But the rhinoceros was too lazy to attack anybody. His skin was thick and his legs were sturdy, and since he would have won a fight with almost any other creature, he never bothered to start one.

So the palace park became home for the animals that were sent to the Queen. After a few years it was teeming with them. There was a pair of water buffalo who spent the whole day churning up and down through the mud beside the lake. Two lions and a black jaguar stalked in a section that had been set aside especially for them. Zebras, antelope and a yellow llama roamed the open ground, looking for the most succulent grasses. There were seven different sorts of monkeys, including two kinds of baboons with faces painted like clowns. Each tribe had its own trees and was always attacking the territory of the others, just like people. There was a moose, which some people called an elk, who completely ignored the monkey wars that took place above his antlers. A very solemn emperor penguin reluctantly shared his pool with a playful seal. There were bats who lived in a cave on the edge of the park, possums and a sleek, shiny mink, who all came out at night. And there were birds...

The birds lived in a gigantic cage that the palace blacksmith had constructed. It was so big that the whole palace could have fitted into it! The Stablekeeper said there were two hundred and eighty different kinds of birds inside, but the truth was that he had lost count and nobody knew for sure. There were parrots, puffins, woodpeckers, nutcrackers, fruitflickers, cockatoos, toucans, lyrebirds, songbirds, mutton-birds, firebirds, lovebirds, rumbirds and at least three hornbills, gigantic black birds from the jungles of the south, with bright faces and a haunting cry that came out of the hollow

horn around their beaks. There were nests in every tree, eggs in every nest, chicks turning into fledglings and fledglings turning into adults. The cage was at the very centre of the park and it flashed with colour and exploded with noise from dawn to dusk.

Of course, the people sent plants as well. They sent seeds and nuts that the Queen's gardeners could grow. They sent bushes and cactuses, they sent whole trees in enormous pots. No matter what time of year it was, somewhere in the palace park you were sure to find a shrub covered in gorgeous flowers or a tree with delicious fruit hanging from its branches. And when a plant would not grow in the palace park, because the weather was too hot or too cold for it, the people sent its fruits for the Queen to taste.

They picked the fruits when they were hard and green, and packed them carefully in boxes lined with cotton wool. By the time they had crossed the sea and arrived at the Queen's palace they were just ripe and ready to eat. This was the Queen's favourite kind of present. There was nothing she loved more than biting into a rich, sweet, delicious fruit that had come from over the seas. The Queen had tasted every fruit that grew in her seven countries, every single fruit except the *melidrop*.

The melidrop was not a particularly large fruit—not much bigger than an egg, or not much smaller than a pomegranate. Its skin went yellow or red as it ripened.

Some people said that its flesh tasted like spicy currants dipped in honey, while some said it was like spicy honey mixed with currants. Others described it as cinnamon custard with walnut syrup. Others who had eaten it refused to say what it was like, claiming that there was nothing else on earth so sweet, smooth and delicious with which it could be compared.

Melidrops grew far to the south, in the hottest of the Queen's countries. Year after year, she heard about these mouth-watering melidrops and waited to taste them.

The people sent melidrop seeds, but they failed to shoot. They sent melidrop trees, but their leaves curled up and died. Then the people tried sending melidrop fruit, but no matter how early they picked them, the fruit always spoiled in the box. The Queen would open the packing case to find a disgusting, smelly pile of darkened melidrop skins.

Sutton Pufrock didn't know why people bothered sending the packing cases, or why the Queen even bothered opening them. On her most recent birthday, while the Queen was still staring at a revolting pile of rotten melidrops that had just arrived, he said: 'It's only to be expected. You have to eat a melidrop the day it's picked. Everyone knows that. That's what melidrops are like. It's a simple fact: after a day, they rot.'

The Queen glared at Sutton Pufrock. The courtiers stared at him as well. They had all come to the palace and were gathered in the Throne-room to watch the Queen open her presents.

'It *is* the most delicious fruit,' Sutton Pufrock continued nostalgically. 'Nothing can compare to it. I remember, when I was younger and far away on my travels, I would sometimes spend a day beneath a melidrop tree, plucking one fruit after another to my heart's content. I would advise anyone who has the opportunity to do the same.'

The Queen shrieked in frustration and slammed the lid of the box. She ordered her footmen to carry Sutton Pufrock away immediately.

It was too much. It was just too much! For years people had been sending her melidrop seeds, melidrop trees and melidrop fruit, and she had still not succeeded in tasting a single one. It was just too humiliating for a Queen to bear.

'That's the end of the matter,' she shouted icily, as Sutton Pufrock's stretcher disappeared out of the Throne-room on the shoulders of the footmen.

The Queen gazed around at her courtiers to see if anyone dared to disagree. They looked back at her blankly. A courtier did not disagree with the Queen, and if he did, he certainly did not show it. Besides, quite a few of them didn't even like Sutton Pufrock and his never-ending travel stories, and they were not sorry to see him go. They waited for the Queen to open the rest of her presents.

But the Queen did not feel like opening any of the other boxes that stood in the Throne-room. She didn't feel like going out into the park to watch her animal-keepers unlock the cages that had arrived, even though one of them was said to contain a strange new animal called a walrus.

'*That* is the end of the matter,' the Queen repeated, just in case anyone had not heard her the first time. 'No one at my Court will *mention* the word melidrop again. Not to me. Not to anyone else. Not to anybody. *Ever*. The melidrop refuses to come to the Queen. Therefore, at the Queen's Court, the melidrop does not exist.'

The Queen glared at everybody a moment longer. Then she turned on her heel and walked out, leaving the footmen to gather up her birthday boxes and run after her.

Chapter 2

It was not the end of the matter.

It was not the end of the matter for one simple reason: melidrops *did* exist. Even if the Queen and the whole Court pretended that there was no such thing as a melidrop, it did not change the fact that there *was* such a thing and that thousands of people, far to the south, enjoyed eating it every day. And *everyone* knew it. Far to the south, people still rested under melidrop trees all day, as Sutton Pufrock had done on his travels, and plucked one melidrop after the other to their heart's content. And there was another fact that it did not change: when you try to pretend that something doesn't exist, you end up spending more time thinking about it than you ever did before.

The Queen could hardly think of anything else. In her mind, melidrops grew and grew, becoming bigger, fresher, juicier, sweeter and tastier by the day. No one mentioned them to her. No one would have dared to whisper the word. But it didn't help. Try as she might, the Queen just couldn't stop thinking about melidrops. They would appear suddenly in front of her, hanging in the air, when she was listening to a boring speech from an ambassador. They turned up on the desk beside her pen when she was signing the Prime Minister's laws. A big orange one even skewered itself on top of her crown and refused to budge, no matter how many times the Queen told herself that it wasn't really there. She was ready to cry with frustration. Was it really possible that she, *the Queen*, would never taste this fruit? Nothing else could give her any pleasure.

Mangoes, pineapples, apricots, bananas, peaches, passionfruit, pomegranates, grapes, blackberries, gooseberries, dates, figs and prickly pears arrived by the crateload, luscious and ripe, but the Queen turned up her nose and told her servants to take them home to their children. The servants' children had never had so much to eat. As far as the Queen was concerned, if it wasn't a melidrop, it may as well be a turnip!

The atmosphere became very bleak at Court. There was hardly any conversation. The Prime Minister came to tell the Queen about an excellent new law that he had invented. From now on, everyone would have to wear a hat between lunchtime and dinnertime, which would make him very popular with all the people who produced hats or sold them in shops. The Queen told him to go away and stop bothering her with his laws and regulations. When the Mayor asked her to come and open a new hospital, the Queen replied sharply that, as a matter of fact, she wasn't feeling too well herself. She didn't dance at the spring ball, she didn't come to the midsummer concert. And as for the travellers whose stories she had loved to listen to so much—she couldn't bear the sight of them! Sutton Pufrock hadn't been seen on his stretcher for weeks. The Court, in fact, was becoming a very dull and gloomy place. All for the sake of a melidrop!

Lord Ronald of Tull had tea with the Queen every Thursday. Lord Ronald had been a great friend of the old King and had known the Queen ever since she was a baby princess. He had always been her closest adviser, helping her with difficult decisions and sharing the wisdom gained from his long experience, and he loved her like a father. Lord Ronald had never seen her so unhappy. One week followed another, and each Thursday the Queen hardly touched her tea. She would raise her cup to her lips, sigh, and put it down again without taking a sip. Lord Ronald could not bring himself to drink his tea either. He could not bring himself to munch a single one of the butter cakes that he loved so much. He was too sad and upset at the sight of the Queen's unhappiness. Eventually he couldn't bear it any more.

'Are you *quite* all right, madam?' he said one Thursday, as the Queen stared vacantly at her cold tea.

The Queen did not take her eyes off the cup in front of her. 'Yes, I believe so,' she murmured tonelessly.

Out of habit, Lord Ronald patted his moustache with his napkin. He had a fine white moustache that collected crumbs whenever he ate, and he often patted it. But there were no crumbs there this time, since Lord Ronald had not touched a single cake.

'I couldn't help noticing—'

'What have you noticed, Lord Ronald?' the Queen asked, looking up at him sharply.

Lord Ronald coughed. 'Madam, I am an old man. When one is as old as I am there is only one thing that brings any pleasure, and that is to see young people who are happy. You, Madam, are not happy. No, you are not. And if there is anything I can do—'

'There is nothing you can do, Lord Ronald! That is the truth, as we both know. To remind me of it simply makes things worse. So let us not speak of it again.'

'No, madam.'

The Queen nodded. She stared at her tea once more. The footman who was standing beside the door watched her gravely. His white powdered wig, which often made a footman look ridiculous, seemed to add to the concern on his face.

'Do you know what your father, the King, would have done?' Lord Ronald said suddenly.

The Queen looked up in surprise.

'Do you know what he would have done?' Lord Ronald demanded.

'Lord Ronald, I thought we were not going to speak of it again.'

'Well, I'll tell you what he would—'

'Lord Ronald! Do not forget to whom you are speaking.'

Lord Ronald had not forgotten to whom he was speaking. But nothing could stop him now. When he had been younger he had been a famous politician, and had given fiery speeches that had gone on for hours. When another person needed his advice, Lord Ronald gave it, whether the other person wanted it or not. And if there was one thing that the young Queen needed now, it was advice: his advice.

'Do you know what he would have done?' Lord Ronald repeated once more as the Queen stared at him, speechless with shock. 'I knew him, Madam, long before you were born! Your father was a wise and careful king.

But no single person can know everything. When your father needed advice, he listened. He found friends who were not frightened to speak their minds, and he listened when they spoke. More than anything else, that was the secret of his wisdom. You, Madam, are not too old to learn. You will never be too old to learn from his example.'

The Queen's mouth hung open. No one had spoken to her like this since the crown had been placed upon her head!

'The King, Madam, never let a matter rest until he had worked it out,' Lord Ronald continued. 'He did not brood or weep. He worked it out, one way or the other, and then he put it out of his mind. Now, if you want a melidrop—'

'Lord Ronald!'

'Melidrop! Melidrop!' cried Lord Ronald. 'There— I've said it. It's just a word. It doesn't bite. Now, if you want a *melidrop*, find a way to get it. Find someone who'll do it. And if there really is no way to get one— put the idea out of your mind once and for all. Don't pretend the thing doesn't exist. Don't stop people talking about it. Don't deceive yourself that others won't enjoy it. They will. Good luck to them! The world won't change. *That* is my advice, Madam.' Lord Ronald drew a deep breath. 'Now you can do what you like with me. You can throw me out like you threw out poor old

Sutton Pufrock, if you like, just because he told you a story you didn't want to hear.'

Lord Ronald sat back and drained his cold tea at a gulp. He glanced at the footman, who could not hide a smile, even though he was not meant to listen to any of the conversations he heard while serving the Queen.

The Queen picked up a slice of heart-shaped butter cake and nibbled it daintily. She ate it slowly. She ate it so slowly that Lord Ronald had already wolfed down two butter cakes himself before the Queen looked back at him.

'Lord Ronald,' the Queen said eventually, 'you speak far too plainly. You speak far too much.' She smiled. It was the first smile Lord Ronald had seen from her in weeks, and it filled him with joy. 'You are the best friend that I have.'

Chapter 3

THE NEXT DAY, the Queen gave instructions that everyone was to gather in the Throne-room. Even Sutton Pufrock was fetched. As they waited, the murmuring of the courtiers filled the room, rising past the chandeliers and right up to the ceiling, where there was a painting of a very large lady riding a chariot through some clouds. They wondered what it was all about. Why did the Queen suddenly want to see them?

At three o'clock precisely, the Royal Usher thumped his cane on the floor. Silence fell. The doors opened, and the Queen entered.

The courtiers moved apart to clear a generous passage for the Queen. She smiled graciously as she passed, without uttering a word. Lord Ronald of Tull watched her from the back of the room. The Queen sat on her throne. She paused for a moment, looking around at the assembled courtiers.

'I have written a poem,' she said.

Everyone stared in bewilderment. No one except Sir Anthony Browne, the Court Poet, knew what to think. But there was no confusion in Sir Anthony's mind. He was livid with rage. If the Queen wanted a poem, she

should have come to him. She had no business making one up herself, no business at all!

The Queen was not known as a poet. Occasionally she sang when someone played the piano, although her voice wasn't really very good. The Queen had been acting so strangely for the last few weeks, some of the courtiers thought that perhaps she had gone completely mad. But she did not look completely mad. She did not look even partially mad. She was sitting perfectly calmly, unrolling a sheet of paper. A moment later she cleared her throat and began to read.

I have had cumquats stewed with raspberries,
  And cherry pie baked for my tea.
I have found that dates and walnuts
  Go together perfectly.
I have had peaches, pears and persimmons,
  And I am never short of plums.
I recall a load of lychees
  That arrived in wooden drums.
I have had mangoes fresh, and mangoes cooked,
  And mangoes lightly spiced.
I have had pineapple and cantaloupe,
  Always thinly sliced.
I have had all these fruits, and more besides,
  But my life is not complete:
For I have never had a melidrop,
  Or three, or four, to eat.

The Queen looked up from her paper. After a few seconds, the courtiers began to applaud politely. Some of them even liked the poem, and wondered if the Queen had any more to read them. Others found that it made them feel hungry, and they couldn't wait to get home and bite into an apple. Only Sir Anthony Browne could not bring himself to clap. It was the worst poem he had ever heard! All about mangoes and chutneys or some such things. There was nothing poetic about it. Nothing romantic. No spring meadows or rosebuds. Who had ever heard of a poem without a meadow or a rosebud in it? And there were hardly any long words, unless you counted 'cantaloupe', which was such a silly word that it didn't really count at all.

The Queen waited until the applause had finished. 'I think it is very sad,' she said, rolling the paper up and handing it to a footman, 'when a Queen feels she must say that her life is not complete. I think it should make her people sad.'

The courtiers frowned. It was turning into a very bewildering afternoon. What did the Queen mean now?

Sir Hugh Lough took a step towards the Queen. Sir Hugh was the most dashing man at the Court. When someone was needed to come forward, it was usually Sir Hugh, even if he did not know what he was coming forward for.

'Madam, come forward for what?' inquired Sir Hugh.

'To get me a melidrop, Sir Hugh. No one has come forward.' The Queen looked around the Throne-room. 'No one,' she repeated, 'has come forward.'

'I have come forward!' declared Sir Hugh, taking another step towards the Queen to prove that he had. 'Madam, I would gladly go——'

'And I, and I,' cried others behind him.

'But...'

'But what, Sir Hugh? It should be so simple, to bring a fruit back for one's Queen, if one were really prepared to try. You simply go and get it! Really, I would be grateful if someone could explain: *what* is the problem?'

'The problem,' cried Sutton Pufrock from the table where his stretcher had been placed, waving his walking-stick impatiently, 'is that it can't be done. Do you know how long it will take to reach the nearest melidrop tree, Your Highness? Two months on the open sea, that's how long. And a month and a half to get back. And the fruit spoils a day after it's picked, no matter how green it is.'

The Queen glared at Sutton Pufrock, who was proving to be most unhelpful when it came to melidrops. She was tempted to throw him out again, and probably would have, if just at that instant she had not caught the eye of Lord Ronald of Tull.

'Pay no attention to him, Madam,' cried Sir Hugh gallantly. 'Allow me to go.'

'Fool's errand,' shouted Sutton Pufrock.

Sir Hugh turned angrily on the old traveller. 'Are you calling me a fool, Sutton Pufrock?'

'You'd be a fool to go,' replied Pufrock. 'To get a melidrop here will take Inventiveness, Desperation and Perseverance. You don't get that at Court, my boy. The only way you get that is from a lifetime of travel and exploration.'

Sir Hugh snorted. 'Surely you don't mean to go yourself, old man. That really would be too much!'

'Old man? *Old man?*' shouted Sutton Pufrock, rising rashly from his stretcher. 'There's a few things an old man can still teach *you*, Hughie Lough!'

Sutton Pufrock hit the ground with his walking-stick and tottered past Sir Hugh, not pausing for breath until he was only a few steps from the throne.

'Your Highness,' said Sutton Pufrock, swaying on his feet, 'I don't know if a melidrop *can* be brought back here. *I* can't think of how to do it, and I've had to think of how to do most things in my time. But if you want it done, there's only one man who's got any hope.'

'And who is that?' demanded Sir Hugh scornfully.

'Bartlett.'

'Bartlett?' asked the Queen.

'Bartlett!' repeated Sutton Pufrock. He raised his walking-stick above his head in his excitement, forgetting that he wasn't on his stretcher anymore. 'Bartlett! Bartlett!' he shouted enthusiastically, and waved the stick wildly in the air.

People ducked and jumped as the walking-stick circled faster and faster above the old man's head. He began to sway. The stick circled, Pufrock swayed more and more. Then he was gone, falling backwards into

29

the arms of a pair of footmen who had rushed forward
to catch him.

'Bartlett's the man,' he said weakly, as the footmen
propped him up. 'I taught him everything he knows.'

'And where is this Bartlett?' asked the Queen.

Sutton Pufrock shrugged. 'Exploring, of course.
Where else would he be?'

Chapter 4

IT TOOK A month just to discover where Bartlett was. It took another month for a messenger to reach him, hanging from a rope above the Piuong Glacier, the most treacherous slope in the Northern Alps. Altogether, it was three months before Bartlett appeared at Court.

But once he arrived he didn't waste a second. Bartlett was not the sort of person to squander his time on long *Hellos* and lingering *Goodbyes*. He went straight to the palace, pausing only to drop in on Sutton Pufrock, who insisted on going with him. But Bartlett wasn't going to wait until the Queen's footmen could be summoned. Together with his companion, Jacques le Grand, he hoisted Sutton Pufrock onto his stretcher and carried him there himself.

Sir Hugh Lough was not impressed. Sir Hugh was never impressed if a man was not dashing, and this famous Bartlett was about as dashing as a milkman. He had freckles on his face and his hair was obviously not very friendly with his comb. His fingers were knobbly. He came to see the Queen in a plain shirt, patched trousers and a pair of worn leather boots that were as creased and creviced as a turtle's neck. And besides, he was thin and wiry. Sir Hugh thought that there was nothing more dashing than a man with bulging muscles. You could see the muscles bulge in Sir Hugh's arms every time he raised a cup to his lips. But Bartlett's muscles were knotted and stringly. Sir Hugh almost pitied him.

The fellow who came with him, however, carrying the other end of Sutton Pufrock's stretcher, was a different type altogether. He was tall and broad. His powerful shoulders were covered by a long fur coat that came down to his knees. He had curly black hair and a broad nose, and he looked around the Throne-room with a simple expression on his face. With a bit of work, thought Sir Hugh, this fellow could be very dashing indeed. He would need some new clothes, of course, and a haircut, and he would certainly need a new expression on his face, something less gentle. But then, thought Sir Hugh, imagining the change, he would be almost frighteningly dashing, almost as dashing—although it was hard to believe it was possible—as Sir Hugh himself!

The Queen was already on her throne.

'Bartlett,' she said, after Sutton Pufrock's stretcher had been put down, 'I am very pleased to see you. We began to wonder if you weren't coming. Step closer.'

She was talking to Jacques le Grand.

Sutton Pufrock cackled with delight. 'The other one, Your Highness.'

'Oh,' said the Queen. 'Are you sure?'

Sutton Pufrock laughed until he almost fell off the table.

'*You* are Bartlett?' the Queen said to the wiry one.

'I am,' said Bartlett. 'They told me I was wanted.'

'Indeed you are,' said the Queen. 'Well, if you really are Bartlett, come forward.'

Bartlett walked closer to the Queen. All around him the courtiers watched curiously, examining him from top to toe. They had never seen anyone approach the Queen in such plain clothes and with such an unprepared appearance.

'Would you like to sit, Mr Bartlett?' asked the Queen,

pointing to a chair that had been placed in front of her.

'No,' replied Bartlett. 'I'd rather stand, if it's all the same to you.'

The courtiers smiled behind their hands. Sir Hugh Lough smirked. It was a very great favour to be allowed to sit in the Queen's presence in the Throne-room. No one ever refused it. It wasn't only Bartlett's boots that needed polishing. His manners could do with some work as well.

'As you wish, Mr Bartlett,' said the Queen. 'Now, the reason I have sent for you is quite simple: melidrops. I want to taste one. I have never tasted a melidrop, and I think it is about time I did.'

The Queen paused, waiting for Bartlett to respond. She was hoping he would say 'That's no problem', or 'I'll just pop out and get you one', or something like that. But Bartlett stared at her silently with a thoughtful expression on his face.

'You do *know* what a melidrop is, don't you?' asked the Queen eventually.

'Of course he does,' shouted Sutton Pufrock merrily, 'he's spent days lying under melidrop trees, picking them to his heart's content.'

'Well?' said the Queen.

'I can get you there,' said Bartlett. 'That's no problem. But I don't see why you needed to send for me. All you need is a sea captain and a ship.'

34

Again there were sniggers in the Throne-room. But Lord Ronald of Tull, who was standing amongst the courtiers, nodded to himself. This fellow Bartlett said what he thought, and meant what he said. Others would have fallen at the Queen's feet and thanked her for summoning them, even if there were no particular reason for them to have been called.

The Queen was beginning to wonder whether it had been worth waiting three months for *this*.

'I can't *go* there!' she exclaimed impatiently. 'You don't understand, Mr Bartlett. I am a Queen.'

'I can see that.'

'Good. Well, now, a Queen simply cannot pack up and go off travelling for months on end. Is that what you think? No, it's quite out of the question. I need someone to bring a melidrop *back* for me.'

Bartlett glanced over his shoulder at Jacques le Grand who replied silently to his gaze.

Bartlett turned back to the Queen. 'Well, you're in trouble. The fruit rots a day after it's picked. Hasn't anyone told you? It's all that sweetness in them. Too sweet for me. Never liked them much myself.'

'I didn't ask you whether you liked them, Mr Bartlett,' the Queen said tartly. 'I didn't ask you to bring one back for *yourself*, I asked you to bring one for me. *I* happen to like melidrops very much indeed.'

'But I thought you said you'd never tasted one.'

The Queen stared rigidly at Bartlett. Sir Hugh Lough all but laughed out loud. Bartlett may have been good at yodelling in the Alps, but he didn't know much about talking to queens.

Lord Ronald smiled. He liked Bartlett's plain speaking more and more.

'Your messenger should have told me what this was all about when he came to get me,' said Bartlett. *'Top secret: For the Queen'*, that's all he'd say. I could have told him then and there and saved us both a lot of trouble. The fruit rots! That's all there is to it.'

The Queen could have shrieked in exasperation. *'I know it rots,'* she exclaimed, forcing the words out between clenched teeth. 'We all know it rots, Bartlett. Even tiny children know it rots. You're not here to tell me that. We want somebody who will find a way to get one back *before* it rots. There is a perfectly able gentleman who was prepared to go three months ago. But Sutton Pufrock convinced me to wait for *you*.'

Bartlett shrugged. 'You should probably send your gentleman, then, if he thinks he can do it.'

'Madam,' cried Sir Hugh in his most dashing fashion, striding forward with a grand sweep of his cape and one hand raised gallantly in the air. 'Have we not seen enough of this man? Allow me to go and I shall soon return

36

with the object of your heart's desire. Just say the word.'

Bartlett glanced at Sir Hugh. 'Is this your gentleman?' he asked.

'It is,' replied the Queen.

'Well, I can see why you didn't send him. Listen, Madam, I can't guarantee that I could get you a melidrop even if I tried, but I can say this: don't trust any man who promises he can. He's a either a liar or a fool.'

Sir Hugh Lough could barely believe his ears. His nostrils flared in rage. *Either a liar or a fool?* The courtiers began to titter. Even the Queen could not suppress a smile.

'Well,' said Bartlett to the Queen, 'if it's all the same to you, I'd best be going. It's a long way back to the Alps.'

He turned to go.

'No!'

Bartlett stopped. The Queen had jumped off her throne. The courtiers had never seen such a thing.

'Mr Bartlett, do you understand? I am asking *you* to go for a melidrop.'

'That's very nice of you, Madam, but Jacques and I, we're not really the right people for the job. You see, we're explorers. Adventurers, you might say. And going for a melidrop, well, it's just a matter of getting a *fruit*, isn't it? Not really a job for explorers like us.'

'But no one has ever brought one back. Isn't that something?'

It was the voice of Lord Ronald of Tull. By now he was convinced that Bartlett was the one for the job. Experience had taught Lord Ronald that a person who at first refuses the flattery of a queen's request is the one who will finally perform it better than anybody else.

'Yes, it is something,' said Bartlett, talking to the old man who had spoken from across the room. 'But it's still only a fruit.'

'Bartlett, I could *order* you to go,' said the Queen, clenching her fists.

'Yes, but you can't order me to succeed,' Bartlett pointed out. 'It will take more than an order to bring back a melidrop, Madam, it will take Inventiveness.'

'And Desperation and Perseverance,' shouted Sutton Pufrock.

'Maybe, Sutt,' said Bartlett, grinning, although he suspected that Inventiveness alone would be enough to bring back a *fruit*.

The Queen slumped on her throne. She couldn't bear to look at Bartlett or Sir Hugh or Lord Ronald, or at anyone, or even to open her eyes, in case she started to see melidrops hanging in the air again. When she discovered that Sutton Pufrock was standing next to her, having left his stretcher and wobbled his way across the floor, she could have reached out and strangled him. After all, it was *his* idea to wait for Bartlett, and she had never met anyone more frustrating in her whole life.

'What do you want?' she hissed.

Sutton Pufrock leaned closer. The Queen stared up in horror as he began to topple towards her. A footman rushed forward and grabbed him just in time. Then he began to speak in a very low tone. No one else could hear what he was saying. The expression on the Queen's face gradually changed. Finally she looked up at the old explorer and nodded with understanding.

Sutton Pufrock shrugged off the footman's arm and wobbled back towards Bartlett.

'Bartlett,' said the Queen, 'Sutton Pufrock has just told me something very interesting about explorers. It seems that the one thing that is certain to make them set off on an adventure, is if they know it will lead to another adventure later on.'

Sutton Pufrock cackled, nudging Bartlett in the ribs.

'So, what is the adventure that you want?'

Bartlett glanced at Jacques le Grand. They both knew, without having to exchange a single word.

'The Margoulis Caverns.'

'The Margoulis Caverns!' cried Sutton Pufrock, whirling his walking-stick and swatting an earring off a lady who was too slow to jump out of the way.

'Are you sure?' said the Queen, wincing as the earring flew over her head and cracked one of the crystals on her chandelier.

Bartlett nodded. The Margoulis Caverns consisted of the longest, deepest chain of caves ever found, with bottomless pools and echoing chambers, but only a fraction of them had been explored. To descend into the earth and map the entire group was one of the great challenges of discovery. They would need a whole team of assistants, equipment, provisions, as well as fourteen mules that had been reared underground and never seen the sun.

'All right,' said the Queen. 'Bring me a melidrop to eat, and I will provide everything you need to make your expedition.'

Bartlett smiled. 'That's very fair, Madam.' He glanced at Jacques to see if he agreed. 'All right, it's a deal.'

The Queen screwed up her nose. She did not make *deals* with people. 'How long will it take you to bring the melidrop?'

Bartlett considered. 'Five months, or seven. Depends if they're in season.'

The Queen stifled a gasp. '*Seven* months?'

'Maybe.'

'Well, since we are making *deals*, Bartlett, if you fail to bring a melidrop, then I *will* send my gentleman. And if I have to send him, the deal is off, and you will get nothing for your expedition. Does that sound fair?'

Bartlett glanced at Sir Hugh, grinning to show that there were no hard feelings. Sir Hugh's nostrils flared again. Obviously there *were* some hard feelings.

Bartlett shrugged. He didn't have the time to worry about touchy gentlemen who couldn't take a joke.

'Very fair,' he said, turning back to the Queen.

'Good. As for getting the melidrop,' said the Queen, motioning to a footman who approached Bartlett with a small leather pouch on a velvet cushion, 'take this purse. Use whatever you need.'

Bartlett took the pouch. He opened it. Rubies and gold coins glinted in the light.

'Is it enough?' asked the Queen.

'More than enough. There'll be plenty of change.'

'Don't worry about the change, Mr Bartlett. Worry about the melidrop.'

Bartlett put the pouch in his pocket and took one last look at the courtiers around him. They were watching him as if he were some kind of strange, scary cat, who might suddenly leap into the air and land on top of them. He turned and marched straight past them to the door.

Bartlett and Jacques stopped as soon as they had crossed the bridge over the palace moat. There was a market there where people sold snacks to courtiers who got hungry while waiting for the Queen. They bought some marmalade buns. Then they sat down on the bank of the moat. Below, frogs croaked in the reeds. Green lilies floated on the water.

'I know,' said Bartlett, 'it's not a proper exploration. It's not even an adventure. But after that—the Margoulis Caverns, Jacques: just imagine! We've dreamed of it for years.'

Jacques le Grand didn't reply. He munched one of the buns. Jacques was one of those people who rarely speak, but for every word that passed his lips he thought ten times as many thoughts as any other person. He and Bartlett had been friends for so long that when Jacques wanted to say something to him, a glance was usually enough. It was Bartlett who did the talking.

'And she *is* spoiled. I know, Jacques; just a spoiled Queen who doesn't deserve our help. Wants to taste a melidrop but can't be bothered to go and get one. And that *gentleman*, Jacques. Have you ever seen a more ridiculous fellow?'

Jacques grinned.

'Just say the word,' Bartlett said very grandly, raising one hand gallantly in imitation of Sir Hugh Lough. 'What word, I'd like to know. Well, we showed *him*, didn't we?'

Bartlett bit into a bun. Jacques began to eat another.

'By the way, Jacques,' said Bartlett, 'I don't suppose you have any idea how to get a melidrop back here?'

Jacques shook his head.

'No,' said Bartlett, 'neither have I.'

Neither did the *gentleman* who had been so ridiculous. But now, as Bartlett and Jacques le Grand walked away from the palace, munching the last of their marmalade buns, Sir Hugh Lough was still fuming with rage. The Queen had left, and all around him in the Throne-room the courtiers were excitedly discussing the two explorers who had *bargained* with her. But Sir Hugh didn't say a word to anyone. Over and over he thought about the adventurer who had dared to approach the Queen dressed like a ragamuffin, and of the way he had insulted him. Even the Queen had laughed, he had seen her. The more he thought, the more his anger grew. Well, there was another lesson that he could have taught Bartlett about life at Court: it was a dangerous things to make an enemy there, especially if you were going on a long journey and there was no one to defend you while you were away.

Chapter 5

BARTLETT AND JACQUES LE GRAND went to the port. They found a ship that was setting sail for the south with a cargo of crockery and linen, and they paid for a cabin with one of the Queen's gold pieces. The voyage took seven weeks, and it would have taken ten if not for the winds that blew in their direction, filling the sails and making them snap and billow. But it was a rocky voyage, with sudden squalls of rain and storms that blew up from over the horizon. The ship pitched and heaved on the waves, rose and fell like a cork. The deck was wet and as slippery as ice and the sailors were tossed from one side to the other as the ship rolled, while crockery cracked with a snap in the hold.

Jacques le Grand suffered badly. In any other situation, he was the strongest and most tireless of companions. He could march for days without sleep, climb a rock face with his bare fingers, haul an entire sled piled high with equipment. But on the open sea, his face went green, his hands went clammy and his stomach churned and heaved. He moaned and groaned with seasickness. When a storm blew up he lay in the cabin, thrown to and fro in his swinging hammock, wishing that the ship

would just flip up and sink to end his suffering.

Bartlett, on the other hand, loved the sea—the rougher the better. Even in the very worst weather he would be on deck with the sailors, lashing down the hatches, or high in the rigging helping to furl the sails. His stringly muscles were tireless, his knobbly fingers gripped the rigging with a tenacious hold and he scampered along the yardarms with the agility of a boy. In the storms, the salt rain lashed his face. The timbers of the masts creaked as if they would split when the ship fell with a stomach-sucking plunge from the top of a towering wave to the bottom of a yawning trough. He loved every minute of it. When he came back to the cabin his streaming oilskin dripped great puddles on the floor while he told Jacques about every hair-raising second.

Jacques would look at him sourly, holding his stomach. 'And did you work out how we're going to bring back a melidrop?' he would ask between groans, just to stop Bartlett feeling too satisfied with himself.

'No,' said Bartlett, 'I still haven't worked that out. But something will turn up.'

It hadn't turned up by the time the voyage ended.

They docked in a busy port. No sooner had the anchor been dropped than men scrambled aboard and began unloading the hold. Other ships stood nearby. There were workers everywhere. They shouted to each other on the quay, swarmed up and down gangplanks, bent double under barrels and crates. Pulleys screeched, wagons rumbled. Out of the ships came cloth, crockery, furniture and metal, and into them went figs, rice, chests of tea, sacks of spices and all the other produce of this rich country.

Bartlett and Jacques le Grand headed straight for the bazaar. There the merchants stood in the shade of brightly coloured awnings, calling to passers-by to sample the excellence of their goods. Mounds of spices, red, yellow, orange and brown, scented the air. Butchers carved, fishmongers filleted, chicken-sellers plucked, crying out and haggling with their customers as they worked. They passed stalls of fabrics, carpets, jewellery, copper; they went past coffee shops and pastry stands and fritter-friers with oil bubbling in seething vats. Then there were rice-sellers, cheese-sellers, sugar-and-honey-sellers, all calling out and beckoning to them. But Bartlett and Jacques didn't stop to sample the goods. They plunged through the crowded alleyways of the bazaar, further and further into its depths, taking one turning after the next, until they found what they were looking for: the Street of the Fruit-sellers, where there was stall after stall of ... melidrops.

The fruit had just come into season and *everyone* was selling them. They were piled high on the stalls, they were in baskets on the ground, blazing orange and red and yellow. Jacques immediately bought a dozen and ate them one after the other as he followed Bartlett between the stalls.

Each melidrop tasted slightly different. Perhaps that was what made them so special. In the bazaar there was a saying: Once you have tasted one melidrop, you are not content until you have another. But it was the melidrop-sellers themselves who had made up that proverb, so it was difficult to say whether it was true.

Bartlett didn't touch a single one. He walked up and down the stalls, eyeing the melidrops suspiciously, as if there must be *one*, somewhere, that could survive, that could cross the sea for six weeks and still be fresh and juicy when it got to the other side. But if there *was* such a melidrop, there was no way of knowing *which* it was.

When the bazaar closed Bartlett and Jacques went to an inn for the night. The whole town was melidrop-mad. The cooks were making melidrop soup, and grilled melidrop with chestnut sauce, and roasted melidrop to go with beef, and sliced melidrop to go in salad, and for dessert you could have baked melidrops or poached melidrops or steamed melidrops or just plain old raw melidrops. At the inn there was a big room with row after row of tables, packed with people slurping melidrop stew and mopping it up off their plates with hunks of bread. The stew came out in a huge black cauldron that was left in the middle of the room and people helped themselves with a ladle. Jacques le Grand went back for seconds. Bartlett stuck to roast lamb and a piece of pumpkin.

'I bet you wish the ship had sunk *now*, don't you?' said Bartlett.

Jacques shook his head energetically, putting a heaped spoonful of stewed melidrop into his mouth.

Bartlett looked around at the people eating furiously. 'All these melidrops, Jacques. It's as if they're mocking us. There must be a way to beat this fruit. But what is it? *What is it?*'

Suddenly Bartlett put down his knife and fork. He pushed his plate to one side and climbed on the table. He clapped his hands twice. Bartlett knew how to get attention. His claps were as loud as explosions.

The clashing of cutlery and the clink of glasses stopped. The room fell silent. Every face was turned towards Bartlett, who was standing high on his table.

'Ladies and gentlemen,' he declared, 'I have come from the Queen!' He paused and pulled the leather pouch out of his pocket. He extracted two large rubies and one gold piece and held them up above his head, turning slowly so that everyone could see them glinting in the light. 'In the Queen's name, I promise *this* treasure to the person who can tell me how to take her a melidrop.'

There was a deep silence. No one in the inn seemed to breathe. All eyes were fixed on the rubies and the gold, sparkling in Bartlett's hands.

Then someone shouted: 'Where is she? Upstairs?'

The room exploded in laughter. People howled in delight. Some of them, who had drunk too much date syrup, laughed so hard they started to cry. Bartlett climbed down. Jacques le Grand, grinning, scraped the melidrop stew off the bottom of his bowl.

The next morning Bartlett said: 'There's no point staying here, Jacques. All they know in town is how to eat melidrops. What we need is someone who knows about *transporting* them.'

They walked back to the bazaar. The melidrop-sellers were hard at work, calling out to the customers who thronged the street.

Bartlett stopped beside a stall that seemed to have especially fresh melidrops. Beads of moisture glistened invitingly on the skin of the fruit. The owner was an old man who wore a tattered cotton cap. He had skin like a lizard and his brown, leathery hands were nimble and practised, pulling melidrops off the stall so fast they seemed to flash through the air.

'Excuse me,' said Bartlett, 'who brings you your melidrops?'

The stall owner glanced suspiciously at Bartlett with his small brown eyes. His hands continued to fly over the fruit, serving a customer.

'Who wants to know?' he asked.

'I do,' said Bartlett.

The man passed a handful of melidrops to the customer and turned to look at Bartlett.

'It's a secret,' he said eventually.

'Why?' asked Bartlett.

'Why? Because for all I know you might want to set up a stall next to mine, and if I tell you who brings my melidrops you'll probably rush off and get them before me. That's why! And my melidrops are the best in the bazaar. Here, taste one.'

The man plucked a bright orange melidrop off the stall and held it out to Bartlett. Bartlett shook his head, but Jacques le Grand accepted it eagerly.

'Mmmmm,' said Jacques, after he had taken a bite.

'See?' said the old man.

'I am *not* here to set up a stall,' said Bartlett.

'Good. Then buy some melidrops and leave me alone. I don't have time to chat.'

'I'm not here to buy melidrops either.'

'Then what are you here for, bananas?'

'The Queen sent me.'

'The Queen?' said the old man. He squinted at Bartlett and rubbed his chin. Suddenly he looked interested. A customer shouted at him but the old man waved her away with his hand as if he were swatting a fly. 'You don't mean that Queen we're always hearing about . . . Where does she live again? . . . Don't tell me, I used to know. Let me think . . .'

'It doesn't matter where she lives,' said Bartlett impatiently. 'She sent me, that's all that matters. And she wants to know who delivers your melidrops.'

'The Queen wants to know who delivers my melidrops? Well, that's different.' The old man looked impressed. Then he glanced suspiciously at Bartlett once more. 'And you're sure you're not going to set up a stall?'

Bartlett shook his head.

'And the Queen isn't either?'

'No! The Queen has better things to do than sell melidrops in the bazaar.'

'There's nothing wrong with selling melidrops in the bazaar!' the old man snapped. He glanced craftily at Jacques le Grand, who had finished his first melidrop and was gazing at the pile on the stall. He picked up another melidrop and put it in Jacques' hand. 'Did the Queen really ask?'

Jacques nodded.

'Well,' said the old man to Bartlett, 'in that case— you've missed him! You can't sleep in if you work in the bazaar, you know. It's not like working for the Queen. He's here by six, gone by eight.'

'What time is it now?' asked Bartlett.

'Ten,' said the old man, 'almost lunchtime! But you might be able to catch him. He takes his wagon to a well outside the town, where his horses drink and rest in the shade until it's cool enough to go home. It's too hot for them to leave any earlier.'

'And where is this well?' asked Bartlett.

'It's on the main road. Just outside the north gate. Anyone will tell you how to find it.'

'And how will we recognise him?'

'His name is Gozo.'

'Gozo?'

'Gozo,' said the old man. 'You'll have to tell him I sent you. He won't talk to you otherwise, because he doesn't want to sell his melidrops to anyone in the bazaar but me. And another thing: don't ask him too many questions. He's very excitable.'

Chapter 6

'*Nine weeks?* Nine weeks, on a ship?' Gozo gave a high-pitched yelp.

Jacques le Grand rolled his eyes. The old man at the bazaar was right, Gozo really was excitable.

'You're crazy, Mr Bartlett! Listen, each day we load the melidrops on the wagon at four in the morning. By seven o'clock, eight at the latest if there are lots of wagons on the road, I deliver them to the old man at the bazaar. He sells them all day and closes his stall in the evening. And the next morning, before I get there, do you know what he does? *He spends an hour throwing out all the ones that are left over from the day before!* They're already starting to rot. And you want to take them for nine weeks! Nine weeks, that's ... sixty ... sixty ...'

'Sixty-three days.'

'*Sixty-three days!* Right. I would have worked it out if you'd given me another minute.' Gozo shook his head, muttering to himself about ships and weeks and sixty-three days, and crazy men called Bartlett. 'Mr Bartlett, you should stop wasting your time. I'm sure there's a ship that can take you home. You've probably got little children who are missing you.'

Bartlett laughed. 'Gozo,' he said, 'I like you.'

Gozo waved an arm. 'Doesn't matter whether you like me, Mr Bartlett. Doesn't matter at all. You're still wasting your time.' And with that Gozo flicked the reins that he was holding, as if to tell his horses what a ridiculous request these two strangers were making.

They had found him at the well outside the north gate, just as the old man at the bazaar had told them. He was lying fast asleep on his wagon in the shade of a tree. A straw hat covered his face. There were at least ten other wagons there as well, each with a sleeping driver. Gozo was the smallest one, no more than a boy. When he woke up and took the hat off his face he didn't look old enough to be driving a wagon. His black hair stood up in spikes, and he had a little upturned nose which made him look even younger.

His uncle, Mordi, had a melidrop farm, and during the melidrop season it was Gozo's job to bring the fruit to the bazaar each morning, except Tuesdays, when the bazaar was closed. On Tuesdays he went home to visit his mother. The wagon he drove was big and creaky, with two shaggy horses to pull it. *That* was the way to transport melidrops, he said. They could come and see for themselves, if they liked. Gozo put on his hat and picked up the reins. Normally he slept for another couple of hours, but he was already awake, and the day wasn't too hot, and the horses had rested. So Bartlett and

Jacques climbed up, dwarfing the little driver between them, and they set off.

They left the well behind. Soon there were rice fields on either side of the road. The bright green of the rice stalks shimmered in pools of water. The road was a narrow track of dazzling white dust. When two wagons crossed, they had to pull to the side and scrape past one another, teetering over the ditches on either side of the road. But Gozo was a skillful driver, and the wagon was always safe.

He drove with his eyes on the road, shoulders hunched, which made him look even smaller than he was. Gradually, remembering the warning of the old man in the bazaar, Bartlett began to question him about transporting melidrops. A wagon could take it eighteen miles, a rider on a fast horse could take it sixty, maybe eighty miles in a day. And how could you take it for nine weeks on a ship? *That* was when Gozo's head jerked up and he yelped excitedly.

It took most of the afternoon to reach Gozo's uncle's farm. The horses walked slowly, having pulled a huge load in the morning, and Gozo didn't hurry them. Jacques le Grand fell asleep and his chin bounced on his chest in time with the wagon's motion. After a while the road left the flat plain and passed between rolling hills, and there were rows of trees instead of rice fields around them. The trees were low, with spreading branches and bright fruit peeping out amongst dark leaves: melidrop orchards. Eventually Gozo turned off the road and took the wagon down an even narrower track, deep into the trees. Branches scraped against the sides of the wagon.

They drew up into a yard. There was a farmhouse, a stable, a barn, and on every side there were the dark leaves and bright fruit of melidrop trees.

The yard was empty. The farmhouse was long and low, and all the shutters were closed. Gozo jumped down and began to unharness one of the horses from the wagon. Jacques le Grand went over to a well near the corner of the farmhouse. He pulled up a bucket of water and drank thirstily. Then he gave the bucket to Bartlett, who tossed it into the well and drew it up again. The door of the farmhouse opened.

A tall man appeared. He had a big bushy beard frizzled with grey. His hair was standing in all directions, as if he had just woken up. He wasn't wearing a shirt, and the pockets on his old trousers were peeling off.

'Uncle Mordi!' cried Gozo, looking up from the harness.

'What's this, have you brought help for the harvesting?' said the man, walking to the well. He glanced at Bartlett and Jacques. Then he picked up a drinking mug that was on the ground beside the well, rinsed it, and filled it with water. He held the mug out to Bartlett.

'Do you need help with the harvesting?' asked Bartlett, taking the mug.

'We always need help.'

'They don't want to help with the harvesting. You won't believe what they want!' shouted Gozo, leading one of the horses into the stable.

'I won't believe it?' said the man, as much to himself as to Bartlett.

Bartlett drained the mug. The water was cool, pure and refreshing. He drank a second mugful.

In the meantime, the man had picked up the bucket and tipped it over his head. 'Aah!' he cried, as the cold water splashed his hair and ran down his back. He skipped and danced on the spot. He shook his head and

58

waved his arms and sprayed water in all directions. 'I love it. Cold water. *I love it!*' he cried, skipping and slapping his chest with his fists.

'They want to transport melidrops,' shouted Gozo, coming out of the stable to get the second horse.

The man gave one last shiver and peered at Bartlett again. He glanced at Jacques le Grand. Drops of water stuck in his beard like glistening berries in a bush.

'You need a wagon,' he said.

'No,' shouted Gozo, 'theydon't want a wagon.'

'Then what do they want?' the man shouted back.

'Ask Bartlett,' shouted Gozo, taking the second horse away.

'Bartlett?'

'Yes,' said Bartlett. 'That's me. And this is my friend, Jacques le Grand.'

Jacques nodded.

'Well, I'm Mordi,' said the man with the bushy beard. 'Welcome to my farm. You know, if you want to transport melidrops the best way really is a wagon. It's very safe, and there's hardly ever—'

'They don't want a wagon!' shouted Gozo, tearing out of the stable, 'I've told you already.'

'Nonsense, Gozo!'

'No,' said Bartlett, 'he's right.'

'See, Uncle Mo, you *never* believe me!' Gozo glared at his uncle with his hands on his hips. He barely came up to Mordi's chest.

Mordi looked down at him. 'What do they want, Gozo?'

'You'll never believe it, Uncle Mo.'

'What?' whispered Mordi.

'Tell him, Mr Bartlett,' said Gozo.

'We want to transport a melidrop—'

'For nine weeks, on a ship!' Gozo blurted out.

'No!' said Mordi.

'Yes!' said Gozo, jumping up and down on the spot. 'Yes yes yes yes *yes!*'

Mordi gazed doubtfully at Bartlett. 'Do you? Really?'

Bartlett nodded.

Mordi glanced at Jacques le Grand to see if it was a joke, but Jacques nodded as well. Mordi frowned for a second. Then his face creased and he began to laugh. The laughter boomed out of his beard, big rolling waves of it, to spread between the melidrop trees in his orchard.

Chapter 7

AFTER SUPPER EVERYONE picked up a lantern to take into the orchard. There was Mordi, his wife, Vara, their five sons and daughters, and three other men who worked with the family during the harvest season. All the melidrops were picked at night. It was the only way to make sure they were still fresh when Gozo delivered them to the bazaar in the morning.

There were harvesting baskets stacked against the wall outside. Mordi bent down and picked up a melidrop that had been left behind in one of them.

'Gozo,' he said. 'Hold up the lantern. Now, Bartlett, this is a melidrop we picked last night.'

Mordi cupped the red—purple fruit in his palm. His fingers were thick and strong, with roughened skin, but he gripped the fruit surprisingly gently, as if it were an egg that might crack in his grasp. Then he pulled out his harvesting knife and quickly slit it down the middle. The two halves fell open on his palm and the yellow flesh glistened in the light.

'You see,' he said, 'it's already going off.'

Everyone peered closely, as if they had never seen a cut melidrop before. Mordi showed the fruit around.

Then he pointed with the tip of his knife to the places where the flesh had already changed from yellow to brown. Just under the skin, in tiny spots, the flesh had darkened.

'You could still eat it now,' he said to Bartlett, 'although an expert could easily tell it was too old. In another six hours, no one would be able to eat it.' He tossed a half of it to his dogs, who sniffed at the fruit and pushed it away. 'Spoiled!' he said, laughing.

Bartlett took the other half of the melidrop. He examined it closely, and handed it to Jacques le Grand. Jacques gave it a quick glance and bit into it.

The other harvesters began to walk away, carrying lanterns and baskets into the orchard.

'Of course, you could take the Queen a *pickled* melidrop,' said Mordi. 'That would keep. We could give you a whole case of pickled melidrops.'

'Don't be silly, Mordi,' said Vara. 'Who wants pickled melidrops when they haven't even tasted fresh ones? What a ridiculous idea!'

Jacques le Grand didn't think it was so ridiculous. A pickled melidrop in exchange for an expedition to the Margoulis Caverns! It seemed an excellent deal.

Bartlett shook his head. 'No, Jacques. I don't think that's what the Queen meant. Vara's right. Pickled won't do.'

'Well,' said Vara, looking around the yard, 'the others

have all started. Come on, Mordi, we'd better get going as well. It's a shame we can't help you, Bartlett. It would be nice to do something for the Queen. Anyway, you'll stay here tonight. Gozo will show you where to sleep, and in the morning he'll take you back to town.'

'Thank you,' said Bartlett.

Vara nodded. She and Mordi each picked up a basket and crossed the yard.

Bartlett, Jacques and Gozo were left by themselves in the darkness. Far off, in the shadow of the orchard, they could see the glow of the lanterns between the trees. They heard the shouts of the harvesters calling to one another. And between the shouts, there was only the silence of the warm night, and the chirping of crickets hiding beneath the house.

Jacques and Gozo went into the farmhouse. Bartlett gazed at the distant lights under the trees. How was it possible to transport the melidrop? No one could tell him. The people who sold melidrops, the people who ate melidrops, and now the people who grew melidrops: none of them knew. If there *was* a way, Bartlett himself would have to invent it.

Gozo woke them at four in the morning. He had already been up for an hour. They followed his candle down the staircase and out into the yard, blinking and yawning. It was still dark. Now the lanterns hung on the wall of the farmhouse. The wagon was piled high with wicker baskets crammed with melidrops, and the horses were already harnessed. The whole family was there, sitting on the ground or leaning against the stable wall, tired out after the night's work.

'All right, Uncle Mo?' shouted Gozo.

'Not yet. We haven't sprayed them.'

Mordi's voice echoed. Bartlett looked for him. Mordi was leaning over the well, hoisting the bucket. When it came to the top he emptied it into a huge brass tin with a spout like a watering can. There was a second watering can next to him, already brimming with water.

Bartlett and Jacques stared at Mordi, wondering what he was doing. They watched as Mordi climbed onto the front of the wagon and raised the weight of the full can with straining arms. He lifted it to the height of his shoulders. Then he tilted it. Bartlett and Jacques saw the water spray out of the spout. The droplets glinted in the light of the lanterns and a mist rose above the dark mounds of melidrops. A shimmering rainbow appeared in it. When the first can was finished, Mordi raised the second and emptied it as well. The melidrops glistened.

'Well,' Mordi said to Bartlett and Jacques after he had climbed down from the wagon, 'it's been a pleasure having you here. At least you've seen a melidrop farm at the height of the harvest. *That's* something to tell the Queen, isn't it?'

Bartlett didn't answer. He was deep in thought, gazing at the glittering droplets that clung to the melidrops. 'Mordi, why did you water the melidrops?' he asked.

Mordi grinned. 'That's our secret. Vara thought of it.'

'Why, Vara?'

Vara shrugged. 'To keep them longer,' she said simply.

'And does it work?'

'Does it work?' shouted Gozo from the wagon seat. *'Does it work!'*

'Our melidrops are the freshest in the bazaar,' said Mordi. 'Ask anyone.'

'Of course, people have found out,' added Vara. 'And everyone does it now. But ours are still the freshest.'

'Come over here,' said Mordi. He led Bartlett to the well. 'Do you remember the freshness of this water? Taste it again.'

Mordi dropped the bucket in the well and hoisted it up. Bartlett dipped the drinking mug and put it to his lips.

The water was pure and cold. Even colder than he remembered.

Bartlett looked down into the well. It was too dark to see the surface of the water.

'Do you know how deep this well is?' asked Mordi. 'Two hundred feet. More. And it goes through *rock*, Bartlett. Hard rock. Cold rock. Rock that has never seen the sun.' Mordi grinned with pride. 'We have the coldest water for miles around. When they're sprayed like that, those melidrops reach the bazaar as fresh as if they've just come off the tree. No one else can beat that!'

Bartlett nodded. He squatted and put his hand in the bucket of water. After a few seconds, his fingers began to go numb.

'It's cold,' said Bartlett.

'It certainly is,' said Mordi.

'Thank you,' said Bartlett.

'What for?'

'You have given me an idea.'

He climbed up onto the wagon beside Gozo, who was ready to go. Jacques climbed up on the other side.

'Thank you,' said Bartlett, to Mordi and Vara, 'for everything.'

'It was nothing,' said Vara.

'No, it was much more than nothing,' said Bartlett, 'much, much more.'

Chapter 8

IT WAS THURSDAY. Lord Ronald of Tull was seated, as usual, opposite the Queen at the small table with the crisp white tablecloth. The Queen handed him his cup. Lord Ronald waited until she had poured her own tea. Then he reached out for a butter cake. Every week, at this precise moment, as the Queen raised her cup to take her first sip of tea, Lord Ronald reached out to take the first of the butter cakes that he loved so much.

The Queen glanced at him. There was a frown on her face. Lord Ronald's hand froze in midair, hovering over the plate.

'Is something wrong, Madam?' he asked in alarm.

The Queen sighed. 'No,' she said, holding her teacup under her chin.

'May I have a cake?' asked Lord Ronald.

'Of course you may, Lord Ronald. What kind of a question is that? You don't need to *ask*.'

'I just wanted to be sure, Madam.'

Lord Ronald picked up a butter cake. The Queen took a quick sip of her tea and swallowed at once, even though the tea was piping hot. She put her cup down and stared at Lord Ronald. She began tapping her fingers on the tablecloth. The diamond rings on her fingers flashed and sparkled.

It was not possible to enjoy a butter cake with the Queen staring and tapping her fingers like that. The flashing lights from her rings were enough to give one a headache.

'Something *is* wrong, isn't it?' said Lord Ronald, putting down his butter cake.

'No, there is nothing wrong, Lord Ronald. I do wish you would stop carrying on like a nanny. I think I am old enough to do without *that* any more.'

Lord Ronald smiled. He raised his napkin and dabbed at his white moustache, gazing thoughtfully at the Queen.

'Oh, Lord Ronald, don't look at me like that.'

'Like what, Madam?'

'Like *that*, Lord Ronald. You know perfectly well what I mean.'

The Queen looked away impatiently. Lord Ronald sipped his tea. The Queen gazed around the room. She tapped her fingers on the table. She tapped her foot against the leg of the chair.

'Where are they, Lord Ronald?' she burst out suddenly. 'Where *are* they?'

'Who? The footmen?'

'No, Lord Ronald! You're being very difficult today. You know perfectly well whom I mean.'

'Bartlett?'

'Bartlett. And his friend ...'

'Jacques le Grand?'

'That's the one. Bartlett and Jacques le Grand. Where are they? Where have they got to?'

Lord Ronald frowned. 'I believe, Madam, they went to get you a melidrop.'

'I know they went to get me a melidrop,' exclaimed the Queen, 'but they haven't come back!'

Lord Ronald sipped his tea thoughtfully. It was true, Bartlett and Jacques le Grand had not come back. But it was not even two months since they had left.

Lord Ronald put his cup down carefully on his saucer. 'Bartlett said it would take five months, or maybe seven,' he said in his calmest and most soothing voice.

The Queen was not soothed.

'Did that include the time it took for him to get here from the Alps?'

'No, Madam, it did not include the time it took for him to get here from the Alps,' said Lord Ronald.

'But that is most unfair. We had to wait four months for him just to get here.'

'Three, Madam.'

'All right. Three, then, if you want to be picky. It was long enough. He should have included that in the time it was going to take him to get the melidrop.'

'He could have done that,' said Lord Ronald, 'but

70

then it would have taken him eight months, or ten.'

The Queen calculated, gazing suspiciously at Lord Ronald. 'Well, it doesn't matter! How long have they been gone already? It must be months. Months and months.'

It was not months and months. The Queen, Lord Ronald guessed, knew this perfectly well, since she counted each day.

'Seven weeks, Madam.'

'Seven weeks? No, it must be more than that. Eleven weeks. Or ten at the very least.'

'Seven weeks, Madam. Seven weeks and two days.'

'So, almost seven and a half weeks. Almost seven-and-a-half weeks, not seven!'

Lord Ronald nodded. The Queen picked up a butter cake and took a swift bite.

The Queen found it very hard to accept that she might be waiting for seven months. She was accustomed to waiting seven seconds, or seven minutes, or seven hours, or, occasionally, seven days, or, very rarely, seven weeks—but seven *months*, that was a new experience for her and she did not find it pleasant at all. Lord Ronald, secretly, thought it might do her some good.

'You will have to wait, Madam,' he said. 'You will simply have to wait.'

'I don't *want* to wait.'

'But you must.'

The Queen picked up her butter cake again. This time she took a dainty nibble out of it.

'Of course, I *could* wait,' she said, suddenly sounding very sure of herself. 'Of course I could. But let us say, Lord Ronald, for the sake of argument, let us say that I wait for seven months—seven whole months—and then Bartlett comes back without a melidrop.'

'That is possible,' said Lord Ronald.

'*Is it?*' demanded the Queen. Her eyes flashed with anger. 'I rather think it would be *impossible*. It would be an impossible situation. To think that a Queen would have waited seven months, which, I believe, is two months longer than a Queen has ever waited before, only to receive nothing at the end of it. No, that would be impossible.'

'Difficult.'

'Difficult. Difficult as well. Impossible things are always difficult.'

'Impossible things are never difficult.'

'Why not?' the Queen demanded.

'Because they never actually happen.'

The Queen stared at Lord Ronald.

'They are impossible, Madam,' Lord Ronald explained.

The Queen continued to gaze at Lord Ronald. 'All right. *Difficult*,' she said eventually. 'I agree. It would be difficult.'

'Indeed it would. But what do you want to do, Madam?'

'Well,' she said, as if the thought had just occurred to her, 'that fellow Bartlett was not very sure of himself. He did not sound as if he *really* believed that he would be able to bring back a melidrop, did he?'

'He was perfectly honest,' Lord Ronald replied.

'Oh, yes, of course. He was honest. Honesty is all very well. One wants to have honesty. But one also wants to have a melidrop! If a man is not very sure of himself, Lord Ronald, he will not try very hard. He will give up at the first setback. He will not try again and again.'

Lord Ronald shook his head. 'Madam, in my opinion you are mistaking honesty for lack of determination. If you ask me, Bartlett will try everything he knows to get you a melidrop. But you must wait.'

'*Must* I?' said the Queen.

'You must, Madam. You have promised.'

'I did not actually promise to wait, Lord Ronald.'

'Madam ...'

'I did not say "I promise". I did not actually say the words, did I?'

Lord Ronald sighed. 'Madam. You are our Queen. You must not forget that you are an example to us all.'

The Queen gazed at Lord Ronald. How she hated it when he said things like that! It was always so hard to have your own way when Lord Ronald was around. And it made no sense, no sense at all, because Lord Ronald was merely a lord, and she, after all, was the Queen.

'And the expedition to the Margoulis Caverns, Madam?' said Lord Ronald after a moment. 'Surely that will make him try.'

'True, but he has already waited years for that. If he doesn't *really* want to get a melidrop he won't mind waiting a few years more.'

'Who says?'

The Queen hesitated. She avoided Lord Ronald's eyes. 'Sir Hugh Lough,' she replied eventually.

Chapter 9

'ICE?' SAID Gozo, grimacing. He took his eyes off the horses and looked up at Bartlett. 'Where can we find some *ice*? Is that what you said?'

Bartlett nodded.

Gozo frowned. They had just turned back onto the main road amongst the melidrop orchards. Dawn was breaking and the sky was becoming light. Ahead of them stretched a long line of wagons, all heavily loaded and heading for the bazaar in town.

'What is it?' said Gozo.

'Ice? It's water that's frozen,' said Bartlett.

'Frozen?'

Jacques le Grand rolled his eyes. He didn't know why Bartlett had even bothered to ask Gozo where they could get some ice. Anyone who lived in a country with snow knew that you could use ice to preserve food, but here, under the tropical sun, it was never cold enough for water to freeze. People wouldn't have any idea what Bartlett was talking about. Jacques himself had once had a similar conversation in another hot country—well, almost a conversation. He had bumped his head against the ceiling in an inn and had called to see if there was any ice to put on the bump. The innkeeper, who had obviously never seen or even heard of ice in his life, looked at him blankly, and it was then that he *would* have had his conversation, to explain what ice was, but Jacques le Grand did not start conversations so frequently that he could afford to waste one on any old innkeeper.

'Gozo,' Bartlett explained, 'when water gets very cold, it freezes. It becomes hard.'

Gozo laughed. 'Water doesn't get hard, Mr Bartlett. Look at the water in Uncle Mo's well. That's cold. I've never drunk colder water in all my life. But it isn't hard.'

'It *does* get hard, Gozo. When it gets very cold—colder than the water in Mordi's well. When it gets *freezing* cold.'

'Water? *Colder than Uncle Mo's?*' Gozo demanded excitedly.

'Yes.'

'Hard?'

'Like a rock,' growled Jacques le Grand.

Gozo hunched his shoulders. He flicked the reins thoughtfully, as if to ask the horses what they made of this crazy story about hard water. But the horses apparently didn't have an answer, because eventually Gozo said: 'I don't know where you can get water that's as hard as a rock, Mr Bartlett. Are you sure it's water? I can get you rocks, if that's what you need. Plenty of rocks.'

'Ice, Gozo. That's what I need.'

'Then I can't help you, Mr Bartlett.'

No one could help them. Ice was as rare in this country as a melidrop in the Queen's palace. Even in the town, no one even knew what ice was, apart from the town's scholar. The scholar spent all day sitting by himself over books in the town's library. No one else in the town ever went to the library or sat over its books, because they had a scholar to do it.

A whole crowd of people took them to the scholar when they discovered that Bartlett and Jacques were looking for something that no one had ever heard of. They pushed and jostled them up the steps to the library, calling out and praising the scholar's wisdom, knowledge and intelligence. 'No other town has a scholar who knows as much as ours,' they cried as they pushed, and they continued shouting until the library doors swung open and their voices dropped to a hush at the sight of the vast room inside.

Every inch of the walls was lined with books. There was a marble floor and a high ceiling held up by a row of columns along either side. In the very centre of the roof was a dome with a circle of windows, and the light streamed down in hazy shafts like golden fingers poking out of the sky. Below it, on a set of soft cushions made of

purple and yellow silk, with books spread out all around him on the floor, sat a young man.

The young man was very plump. He wore a flowing gown and a soft red hat that flopped like a melted mushroom. On either hand, amongst the books, was a small wooden table, and on the tables were trays of tidbits and delicacies. The scholar held a sweet between his fingers and was just putting it to his mouth when he heard the door of the library open.

He looked up in alarm at the crowd coming towards

him. Although they barely dared to speak above a whisper, in the silence of the library their voices sounded like a tremendous din. Even the sound of their feet shuffling over the marble floor was deafening. The scholar could barely believe his ears. People were not meant to come and make a din in the library! They were supposed to tiptoe in with his food, place it quietly on the tables, and slip away before he had even looked up from his books and realised they were there.

'Ask him, ask him!' whispered the people around Bartlett.

'What?' asked the scholar impatiently.

'We are looking for ice,' said Bartlett.

'Ah, ice!' said the scholar. He held one finger meaningfully in the air. *This* was a question worthy of his great learning.

The people around Bartlett stared at the scholar with their mouths open, barely daring to breathe.

'Ice,' the scholar repeated. 'Water.'

'Yes,' said Bartlett.

'*Frozen* water.'

'Yes,' said Bartlett.

People started clapping. 'You see, you see,' they cried excitedly.

'Wait!' Then, when everyone was quiet again, Bartlett said: 'Where can we find it?'

The scholar's face became troubled. He glanced

around the library, as if the answer must have been inside one of all those books that he had read. The answer to every single question that could possibly be asked, the scholar believed, was inside one or other of his books, if only he could remember which one.

Eventually the scholar shook his head. 'I don't know,' he confessed.

'Thank you,' said Bartlett. He turned to leave. Jacques le Grand followed him out. People were crying 'Food, food! Bring food so the scholar will have strength to learn.'

Gozo ate lunch with Bartlett and Jacques le Grand in an inn. He had left a boy watching his wagon behind the bazaar. Gozo looked unhappy and didn't eat very much.

'What are you going to do, Mr Bartlett?' he asked, pushing a piece of chicken aimlessly around his plate with a fork.

Bartlett smiled. 'I don't know, Gozo. Something always turns up.'

'Not always,' said Gozo.

Bartlett didn't reply. He always said that something would turn up, but it was true that sometimes it didn't. Yet that was no cause for dismay! Inventiveness, Perseverance and Desperation: those were the tools of an explorer. If something didn't turn up by itself, Inventiveness would make it appear!

Gozo frowned. 'You can't find any ice, whatever that is.'

'Not here,' said Bartlett.

'Why don't you bring it, then?'

Jacques laughed. He shook his head merrily before placing a heaped spoonful of meat, potatoes and cabbage into his mouth. The whole lot was covered in spicy melidrop sauce, of course.

'Ice . . .' said Bartlett—then he paused, as if a thought had just come into his mind.

'. . . melts,' Jacques growled, completing Bartlett's sentence out of the corner of his full mouth.

'Yes, it melts,' said Bartlett. But he was still thinking. 'It melts slowly, doesn't it, Jacques? And the more you've got, the slower it melts.'

Jacques didn't care how quickly ice melted. There wasn't any here. And the sooner Bartlett gave up this whole melidrop idea, the better. Bringing a fruit for the Queen was no job for explorers like them, even if she did offer an expedition to the Margoulis Caverns as a reward.

'What do you mean, *melts*?' Gozo asked.

'What? Oh, when it gets warmer, it melts,' said Bartlett. 'Then it's just water again.'

'Then I don't see why you want it. *I don't see at all!*' cried Gozo. 'Water that's hard one minute and soft the next, what's it for? What could you possibly do—'

'Gozo,' cried Bartlett suddenly, 'we have to find a ship!'

'When?'

'Now! Right now!'

Bartlett was already on his feet. He had an expression of wild impatience on his face. Jacques knew that look. When Inventiveness strikes, no explorer can wait to put his idea into action.

They went straight to the port. There were six empty ships waiting for wares to take across the sea. One of them was the ship that had brought Bartlett and Jacques two days before. When Bartlett told the captain what he wanted, the captain laughed in his face. When Bartlett offered him half-a-dozen of the Queen's rubies, he just laughed even louder. So did the captain on the next ship they visited, and the captain on the ship after that. But the fourth captain looked Bartlett up and down, without even waiting to hear about the rubies, and said, 'Maybe.'

'Maybe?' cried Bartlett. 'I don't want maybe. Anyone can say maybe. I want to hear yes. Yes, that's what I want to hear.'

'All right: yes,' said the captain, who was called Captain Wrick.

For a moment Bartlett was silent. He gazed into Captain Wrick's sea-blue eyes. 'Really? Do you think you can do it? Do you think you can bring back an iceberg?'

'Maybe,' said Captain Wrick.

'Well, when will you know for sure?' demanded Bartlett.

'When we get there.'

'Where?'

'To the icebergs.'

'How long will it take?'

'Six weeks.'

'There and back?'

'Each way.'

'Twelve weeks,' muttered Bartlett. 'Gozo, will the melidrops still be in season in twelve weeks?'

Gozo narrowed his eyes. 'That's eighty ... eighty ...'

'Eighty-four days,' cried Bartlett impatiently.

'I know,' said Gozo, 'I would have worked it out.'

Gozo started counting on his fingers, whispering numbers under his breath. No one knew what he was counting. He went round and round his fingers.

'Yes,' he said eventually. 'But that's such a long time, Mr Bartlett. Eighty-four days, that's ... that's ...'

'Twelve weeks.'

'Twelve weeks! Won't the Queen get sick of waiting?'

Bartlett laughed. Getting an iceberg would take extra time, but Bartlett wasn't the sort to count pennies or add up weeks. When you decided you were going to do something, you kept going until you succeeded, no matter how long it took! 'The Queen will wait, Gozo. She promised she would. When a Queen promises something, you can trust she'll do it.'

Jacques raised an eyebrow doubtfully. The Queen had not struck *him* as a particularly patient person.

'Well, they won't be the best melidrops, Mr Bartlett,' said Gozo. 'It'll be the end of the season.'

Bartlett shook his head dismissively. 'We can't worry about that. If the Queen wants a melidrop she'll just have to take what she's given.' He turned back to Captain Wrick. 'When can we sail?'

'Tonight,' replied Captain Wrick.

'What about this afternoon?'

'If you like, I just have to buy some candles.'

'And rope,' added Bartlett, 'for the iceberg.'

'Oh, I've got rope,' said Captain Wrick.

'Good,' said Bartlett. 'Now listen, Gozo. We'll be back in twelve weeks. And as soon as we arrive, you must bring us the freshest, plumpest, juiciest melidrop you have. Make sure Mordi sprays it well before you bring it—no, better yet, put it in a bucket of cold water and bring it in that. As fast as you can. All right?'

'But how will I know when you're back?' asked Gozo.

'Oh, you'll know. We'll be towing the most amazing thing you've ever seen in your life. Ice.'

'Ice?' repeated Gozo, scarcely daring to believe it.

'A whole lump of it, a whole mountain of it. As white

as snow.' Bartlett laughed. 'I suppose you don't know what that is, either. We'll be towing a mountain of ice or we'll have sunk trying to get it. Either way, we won't be back without it. Right, Jacques?'

Jacques nodded glumly. Six weeks there and six weeks back: the mere thought of it was enough to make him seasick!

Chapter 10

SEA CAPTAINS DON'T normally go looking for icebergs—
they steer as far away from them as possible. The underwater part of an iceberg is like a razor-sharp claw that
can rip the bottom out of a ship, and the part above
water will smash a boat to pieces if they collide in a
storm. Captain Wrick knew all of this. He didn't say yes
to Bartlett out of ignorance.

Captain Wrick had been at sea for over forty years,
starting as a boy of eleven. His cheeks were rubbed red
by the sea wind and his beard was as white as the sea
spray. He had seen almost everything, and done almost
everything there is to see or do at sea. He had been cabin
boy, midshipman, first mate and skipper. He had sailed
with spices, carried coal, traded timber and transported
ambassadors on secret missions. He had been sunk,
shipwrecked, captured by pirates, caught up in sea bat-
tles and driven onto coral reefs by tropical storms. He
was always calm. That was his secret. He was always
steady. He never threw things around in a temper and
he never whooped with delight. His First Mate, Michael,
who had sailed with him for seventeen years, had never
heard him raise his voice. Captain Wrick had seen and

done so much that there was virtually nothing left that could surprise him.

But he had never towed an iceberg. He had never even heard anyone say that they wanted to do it. It was the strangest idea he had come across for years, and it was a lot more exciting than sailing with yet another load of figs across the same seas to the same ports that he had visited a thousand times already! But could it be done? That was the question. He was curious. When this wiry man and his big friend arrived on his ship and asked if he would do it, a voice inside him said: 'Wrick, you must find out.'

To be frank, he did not really know if it was possible, but if there was any ship that could do it, his own vessel, the *Fortune Bey*, was the one. The *Bey* had three tall masts, a stout rudder and decks of seasoned wood. The figurehead that jutted forward from its prow was in the shape of a man wearing a golden turban and a fierce moustache. Captain Wrick had sailed the *Bey* for years

and knew every creak of its timbers. It was like an old friend and the sturdiest of companions.

The captain's cabin was at the back of the *Bey*, with windows of thick glass that looked out over the rudder and the churning wake in the sea. In one corner there was a simple sailor's hammock, where Captain Wrick slept. Near the windows there was a table covered in maps and sea charts, as well as the compass, telescope, sextant and other instruments that a captain requires. A

lantern hung from a beam above the table, and the whole place smelled of beeswax and warm tobacco from the pipe that Captain Wrick smoked. He smoked it as he sat with Bartlett at the table for hours and hours on the six-week journey to the ice seas, trying to work out how to tow an iceberg. Jacques le Grand joined them whenever he wasn't feeling too seasick, and sometimes the First Mate, Michael, came in to add his ideas, leaving the second mate to steer the ship.

At first they thought of simply throwing a great loop of rope around the iceberg and towing it like that, but everyone soon realised that the loop would slip over the iceberg's tip as it began to melt. Then Bartlett thought of using a chain, because that would bite into the ice, but a chain would fall and sink as the ice melted. Then they thought of cutting a groove into the ice so a rope wouldn't slip off, but of course a groove would melt away as well, and then they thought of using a chain *in* a groove, but that wasn't any better ... The days passed, the lantern swayed from the beam above their heads, and their ideas went round and round in circles, trying to work out how an iceberg might be towed.

Of course, that wasn't the only problem. How large should the iceberg be? It needed to be big, because as soon as they took it into warmer waters it would start to melt. It had to last not only long enough to get back to

Gozo, who would give them a melidrop, but then to make it all the way back to the Queen as well. Yet the bigger the iceberg, the more slowly they would travel and the more time it would have to melt before they finished their journey. And if it was *too* big, they wouldn't be able to tow it at all.

Captain Wrick, who was an expert on everything that was known about the sea, spent whole days making complicated calculations to work out the size of the iceberg they should take. One day he concentrated on the speed of the wind, the next day it was the strength of the currents. Then there was the temperature of the water, the weight of the ship, the height of the waves, the shape of the iceberg, the amount of rain, the strength of the sun, and every time he sat down to work it out he thought of something else. Eventually he tried to put everything together in one big formula. Then he gave up.

'We'll have to see when we get there' he said. 'I think I can make a good guess of the size we can manage.'

But it turned out that Captain Wrick did not make a good guess of the size they could manage. It had never been done before, and he had no experience. By now they had been at sea for over five weeks. They were entering the freezing ocean. The air was cold; icicles sprouted on the rigging. On deck, the sailors slipped on frozen puddles. Their breath turned to ice in the air. The sea mists reached down to the very bone and chilled the marrow, and even when the sun shone there was no warmth, but only the glitter of frost on the ship's timbers. A few days later they began to see icebergs.

The icebergs were gigantic. They rose out of the sea like white cliffs. Captain Wrick sailed carefully amongst them, keeping as much distance as he could. Finally he made for an immense mountain of ice that stood twice as high as the ship's main mast. He ordered the sails to be furled. A cold sun was shining and the sea was as blue and as still as freezing metal. The *Fortune Bey* stood motionless on the water. Captain Wrick went below with Bartlett, Jacques and Michael. Outside the cabin window, the iceberg loomed silently, reaching into the sky and dazzling the eyes with its whiteness, dwarfing everything.

'It'll be easier to tow than it looks,' said Captain Wrick.

Bartlett glanced at the iceberg. It couldn't be harder to tow than it looked—it looked impossible.

'I'm certain,' said Captain Wrick, 'I've done all the calculations.'

The calculations were on the desk—pages and pages. But no one examined them. There was still the other problem they hadn't solved: how would they tow it?

'Shall we try the rope?' said Michael.

They all gazed at the huge bulk of the iceberg. No one could imagine getting enough rope around that monster to be able to tow it.

'The chain?'

There was the same problem with the chain.

'You know, we used to tow whales with chains,' said Michael, 'when I worked on a whaling ship. We used to put the chains around their tails and—'

'Whales?' said Bartlett suddenly.

'Yes. We used to put chains—'

'What about harpoons?'

'No, Bartlett,' said Michael, glancing at Captain Wrick with a grin, as if to say how little explorers knew about the sea. 'You kill the whales with the harpoons, then you drag them with chains.'

But Bartlett wasn't listening. 'Captain Wrick,' he cried, 'have we got harpoons?'

'Bartlett, the iceberg isn't *alive*. We don't need to kill it.'

'I don't want to kill it. But I want harpoons. Do we have any?'

'Yes, but—'

'Good! Let's have them. Three. And three long chains. And we'll need a hammer, from the carpenter— the biggest he has!' Bartlett grinned. Captain Wrick and Michael were staring at him in confusion. 'Don't worry, you'll understand soon enough,' he said, and he turned to Jacques. 'Come on, Jacques, that iceberg won't wait forever!'

A boat was lowered. Bartlett and Jacques jumped in and rowed to the iceberg. The whole crew was on deck to see what they would do. And it was very simple: Jacques raised the sledgehammer and, using his enormous strength, drove the harpoons into the side of the iceberg. The ice splintered and flew as the stakes went in. Then Bartlett attached a chain to each one. Then they rowed back, bringing the other ends of the chains with them to fasten to the stern of the *Fortune Bey*. And now the iceberg was securely attached. The *Bey* was ready to tow it.

But it didn't. For a day and a half the ship sat absolutely still in the water. Even when the breeze picked up and the sails billowed and filled with air, the *Bey* didn't move an inch. It was simply unable to shift the monstrous iceberg. And so everyone began to wonder—if the ship couldn't move the iceberg, did that mean that the iceberg could move the ship? The answer came on the second day. The wind changed direction. The iceberg began to drift. But it wasn't following the *Bey*: the iceberg was moving backwards, and the *Bey* was following *it!*

The *Fortune Bey* began to pick up speed. The iceberg began to rock, and every time it rocked the ship rolled wildly to the side. Captain Wrick gripped the wheel, gazing determinedly across the water. His face was calm but his lips were pressed together and they were going whiter and whiter. The iceberg rocked again and the ship pitched once more, going over almost completely on its side. The sailors held on grimly and gasped as the freezing water of the waves crashed across them.

'Release the chains,' Captain Wrick murmured to Michael.

'Release the chains!' Michael roared, and three men scrambled towards the stern.

The chains came free with a snap. They whipped loose and their ends flew into the air.

The *Fortune Bey* lurched for a while longer. The gigantic iceberg continued to drift. Soon it was far away, with the harpoons still in its side, like three tiny needles sticking into the vast bulk of an elephant's skin.

Chapter 11

ICEBERGS FLOATED ALL around, like gigantic white beasts asleep in the water. When would they awake? In the sunlight their whiteness sparkled, dazzling the eyes. When there was a mist they emerged like the silent ghosts of sunken ships. On clear nights the moonlight slipped off them as if they were made of green glass.

For a week the *Fortune Bey* sailed amongst the slumbering white giants. The sailors huddled in their cabins or drank mugs of scalding tea in the galley. Only those who were needed for a job went above deck. Water froze and the air was icy. Captain Wrick began to wonder whether the time had come to sail out of the freezing seas, admitting defeat. The icebergs were enormous, they could never hope to tow them. Always there was the danger of seeing one too late in a fog, or of being thrown against one by the wind. And sooner or later there would be a storm. Then the silent, white beasts would awaken. The wind would howl and their great white bodies would pitch and shudder in the waves, crushing anything that crossed their paths.

It happened that night. A claw of ice tore at the heart of the *Fortune Bey*.

It began with a terrible screeching, as if the very timbers of the *Bey* were in agony. Captain Wrick sat bolt upright in his hammock. Bartlett and Jacques le Grand awoke with a jolt. All over the ship, sailors opened their eyes in the darkness, their stomachs knotted at the sound. They jumped up and ran out of their cabins, not even stopping to throw on their shirts, pouring up the stairs and onto the freezing deck, where they stopped, aghast, at the sight that met their eyes: a wall of ice standing in the mist not more than a mast-length from the side of the boat, and the *Bey* scraping across the long jagged shelf of ice that stretched underwater.

The screeching went on and on. The *Bey* was moving slowly. The ice scratched and tore at it. The sailors stood transfixed, as if unaware that they were freezing, as if the noise itself nailed them to the spot. Then all at once Captain Wrick's voice was heard, calm, steady but desperate, ordering the men across. *Across!* Across to the other side of the ship, where their weight might help to dip the *Bey* and release it from the ice. Men ran, slipping and sliding over the frozen deck. Bartlett and Jacques ran as well with all the Desperation in their bodies. 'Across! Across!' came Captain Wrick's voice, and now it was close to them, because he had run across as well, with every sailor that was on the ship.

Still the timbers of the *Bey* shrieked. Now the men could only listen and watch, waiting for the *Bey* to pass the iceberg and hoping they would still be afloat at the end of it. They stared at the wall of ice as the ship moved slowly along it. Every screeching of the timbers was like a knife plunging into their bellies. Some held their breath, some mumbled prayers. None dared to look away from the iceberg, as if it held them all in its power.

The screeching stopped.

Suddenly there was silence. It seemed so deep that it could scarcely be real.

The *Bey* pitched, rolled a little, then straightened.

Still hardly anyone dared move. What would happen now? The iceberg had disappeared into the mist from which it came. Was the ship filling with water under their feet? What was left of the timbers of the *Fortune Bey*?

The *Bey's* life did not end that night. The ship was wounded, but not killed. They found a small leak near the prow, and the carpenter repaired it. The sturdy timbers of the *Fortune Bey* had saved them all. But if the water had been a couple of inches shallower, or if the ice had been a tiny bit more jagged, or if the *Bey* had not dipped when the men moved to the side, then the entire bottom of the ship would have been left behind. This time it had survived. But if they stayed in the freezing seas, Captain Wrick knew, another of the white beasts would eventually claim it.

That morning, Captain Wrick told Bartlett and Jacques le Grand that he was turning back. He didn't say it sadly or happily. He said it in his usual calm, steady way, just as he had told Bartlett that he would take him in the first place. Bartlett nodded. There was no point arguing. Captain Wrick had said that he would try to get an iceberg, and he had tried his best. There was no point offering him more of the Queen's rubies and gold coins to persuade him to change his mind.

Jacques didn't try to persuade him either. After all, if they didn't get an iceberg, they could finally forget all about this ridiculous idea of taking a melidop to the Queen.

'All right,' Bartlett said to the captain. 'But it's still possible we'll find an iceberg that's the right size.'

'I'm not going to look for any more, Bartlett. We're turning back.'

'No, but we could find one on the way.'

Captain Wrick smiled. 'It's not very likely, you know. But if we do find one, we'll take it. I didn't risk my ship for nothing, Bartlett. I want one as much as you.'

'I know.' Bartlett got up.

'Where are you going?' asked the captain.

'To the crow's nest.'

'There's someone there already, Bartlett. Stay here where it's warm.'

Bartlett shook his head. There was always someone in the crow's nest at the top of the mast, but it was a monotonous job and the lookouts did not necessarily pay as much attention as they should. For example, they could easily miss a medium-size iceberg that was far away on the horizon, where it would look no bigger than a dot.

Bartlett left the cabin. He climbed the mast. He was beginning to think he had been wrong about getting a melidrop. He thought it would require only Inventiveness, but last night they had also needed Desperation to survive. Now Bartlett had a feeling that it would require Perseverance as well.

Chapter 12

FROM THE CROW's nest, the sea looked like a vast blue plate, dotted with gigantic white icebergs in every direction. Bartlett looked down and saw Captain Wrick on the bridge, spinning the wheel with both hands. Bartlett felt the mast sway. The *Fortune Bey* was turning. The sailors had been sent aloft and now they were out on the yardarms, working at the rigging. Like a host of butterflies opening their wings, one after another, the sails dropped open, flapped, and snapped stiffly as the breeze filled them. The *Fortune Bey* began to gather speed.

From now on, Bartlett gazed only into the distance, scanning the ocean ahead.

After a couple of hours the lookout was replaced by another sailor.

He brought a mug of hot tea, which he carried in one hand as he climbed the rope ladder up the mast. The tea helped warm Bartlett up. High in the crow's nest, the wind was even more freezing than on deck, and not even a scarf could keep your nose from turning to ice. It was so cold that each lookout stayed for only two hours before being replaced. But Bartlett persevered. Throughout the day the lookouts came and went while Bartlett scanned the horizon.

The next day he was back in the crow's nest, and he was there again the following day, and on the day after that. By now the *Fortune Bey* was leaving the freezing seas behind. The air was not so bitingly cold, the water no longer froze on the deck. There were fewer and fewer icebergs, but each one that Bartlett saw was still too large to tow. On the next day he did not see a single one.

'I'm sorry,' said Captain Wrick at dinner that night, 'but we did try.'

Jacques le Grand shrugged his shoulders. He was sick of being cooped up in a cabin. He was sick of the salty air. He was sick of being too seasick to eat and of eating mouldy ship's food when he wasn't. He wanted to get his feet on dry land, a good meal in his belly and a plan for some real exploration in his head. Back to the Alps— that would be good enough for him!

Bartlett didn't say anything. There was nothing for

Captain Wrick to be sorry about. And as far as he was concerned, no one had stopped trying. At least, *he* hadn't.

The next day Bartlett was back in the crow's nest and he was there the following day as well, and every day for the next week, even though they were already back in a warmer climate and some of the sailors had started taking off their shirts when they were working on deck. Altogether he would probably have spent the whole journey back, all six weeks of it, in the crow's nest, if not for the fact that on the morning after *that*, as he was scanning the ocean, he noticed something unusual: a tiny white dot on the horizon.

At first he wasn't sure if his eyes were playing tricks. Staring at the ocean for day after day, it was possible that you began to see things. He looked away, looked back, blinked, looked away again, but whenever he looked back the white dot was still there. And as they sailed towards it, it was getting bigger. By the middle of the afternoon there was no longer any doubt: it was an iceberg, floating far from the freezing seas.

Bartlett dropped down the mast as fast as his limbs would take him. He found Captain Wrick in his cabin and a moment later he was on deck with his telescope to his eye. He gazed for a full minute at least. Then he turned to Bartlett with a real grin on his face. Michael, who was watching, was quite shocked at seeing so much joy in his captain's expression.

'Well,' said Captain Wrick, 'you were right, Bartlett. I'd given up hope.'

'Perseverance, Captain Wrick,' said Bartlett, winking at Jacques le Grand.

Captain Wrick shook his head in amazement. 'There are stories about these icebergs. A current gets hold of them and drives them north. It takes them months to melt and they usually end up sinking a ship that isn't expecting them. But I've never seen one myself.'

Bartlett took the telescope. 'It doesn't look too big. But is it too *small?* Will it last?'

Bartlett, Captain Wrick and Jacques stared at each other. None of them knew.

Bartlett grinned. 'There's only one way to find out!'

Captain Wrick allowed himself a second smile. 'Set the course, Michael.'

Jacques stared at the iceberg as Michael turned the wheel. 'I hope the Queen's prepared to wait,' he muttered.

Bartlett and Captain Wrick looked at him in surprise.

'I hope she's prepared to wait,' Jacques repeated. 'She sits there in her palace and thinks it's just a matter of snapping her fingers and telling people what to do—and everything will happen, just like that! Do you remember, Bartlett? Seven months was too long for her! Well, we almost drowned last week, a whole shipload of us, for the sake of a *fruit*.' Jacques nodded fiercely to himself. 'I just hope she's prepared to wait.'

Bartlett frowned. That was one of the longest speeches Jacques had ever made. What a strange topic for him to choose! After a moment, he almost laughed out loud.

By the end of the afternoon they had reached the iceberg. The *Fortune Bey* rode at rest not more than a chain's length away. It was about a third of the size of the iceberg they had first tried to tow. On one side it had a sharp peak, almost as tall as the mast of the *Fortune Bey*, and on the other side there was a flat bed of ice that rose only a few feet above the water. The iceberg had probably come from a larger block that had fractured in two.

Once again, Bartlett and Jacques le Grand took a boat with harpoons and chains. Jacques drove the harpoons into the ice. After they returned to the *Bey*, the three chains were bolted to the stern. The sun had just started to set. Captain Wrick ordered the sails unfurled. A brisk breeze was blowing. The sails snapped, billowed and bulged with air.

The *Fortune Bey* began to move with the winds. As the ship moved, the three chains rose out of the water. They stretched taut. The *Bey* creaked and stopped.

Bartlett held his breath. This was the last chance. To

find an iceberg here was a freak. They wouldn't find another.

The *Bey* shuddered. The wind blew. The turbaned figurehead at the prow quivered, almost as if he were grimacing with the effort. Finally, more slowly than before, the *Fortune Bey* began to move—and the iceberg, like a reluctant captive, began to follow.

Bartlett stood at the rail at the very back of the ship. The sun was a red disc on the horizon, plunging into the sea. The air had grown cool and the blue of the sky was deepening into black. In the wake of the *Fortune Bey*, the iceberg floated, led by the three chains that pricked its side.

Suddenly a seal put its head out of the sea. It bobbed in the water. Then as Bartlett watched, it crawled onto the ice. It wriggled its flippers. Bartlett smiled. The iceberg had a guest. Soon another seal followed, and then others arrived, clambering out of the water. Bartlett continued to watch even when it was too dark to see anything but a reflection of the light of the first evening stars, and the seals had become black blotches on their dark bed.

Still Bartlett could not tear himself away. The iceberg was so white, so pure, so hard. It could be a home for seals. It could sink a ship. And now, hoping to deliver a melidrop to a Queen, they were going to take it into the warmth, where it would melt and disappear.

Chapter 13

SIR HUGH LOUGH was standing under one of the exotic trees in the palace park. The Queen was having one of her garden parties and the animals, which had been herded away to the bottom of the park for the day, were replaced by people in their finest clothes. They stood around with cups of tea and dainty sandwiches distributed, by servants, from silver trays.

'Well, James,' muttered Sir Hugh to the man who was standing beside him, 'perhaps the time has come to see whether her patience has finally broken.'

'Whose patience?' said Sir James.

Sir Hugh sighed. Sir James Finague was not a very clever man. He was also not very dashing. He was slim, delicate and pale, with long teeth and carefully shaped fingernails, and there was something about him that reminded Sir Hugh of a rabbit, always ready to hop away at the first sign of trouble. In fact, Sir Hugh did not even like him. But Sir James liked *Sir Hugh*, and would do almost anything to be seen with him. And at Court, where there were always others who wanted to spoil one's plans, people like that could be very useful.

'The Queen!' said Sir Hugh impatiently, and he

nodded towards her. She stood in the distance, not far from the birdcage, talking to a group of courtiers.

'I see,' said Sir James. 'Well, she *did* say she would wait.'

Sir Hugh laughed out loud. 'Wait? *Our* Queen? Seven months?' He glanced at Sir James, shaking his head with amusement.

Sir James grinned sheepishly.

Sir Hugh turned back to look at the Queen. Day by day, week by week, he had watched her frustration increasing. Now and again, at the right moment of course, he had said something to help it along. For instance, Bartlett, after all, had already waited years to explore the Margoulis Caverns. Wouldn't he be prepared to wait a few more? For example, Bartlett was not necessarily a man you could trust. Who knew him apart from Sutton Pufrock? For instance, Bartlett did not necessarily care about the Queen. Did he seem like the sort of man who would risk life and limb for her? Yes, the right word at the right time could raise all sorts of doubts. And the Queen's patience, which was never very strong, was stretching thinner and thinner. Perhaps, with one last push, it would snap.

Sir Hugh stepped out from under the tree. Sir James scampered to keep up with him.

'When I nod,' murmured Sir Hugh, 'say something about how long it's taking to get the Queen's melidrop.'

'You mean, something like: "It's taking a long time to get the Queen's melidrop"?'

'Perfect,' said Sir Hugh. He stopped not far from the Queen. If one spoke loudly, she might almost be able to hear, even over the noise of the birds behind her. At once a crowd of ladies and gentlemen gathered around him, eager to be seen with the most dashing man at Court. A servant came with tea and sandwiches. A moment later, Sir Hugh nodded at Sir James.

'Do you know,' said Sir James to the woman standing beside him, with a tremor in his voice because he knew that Sir Hugh was listening, 'it's taking rather a while … I mean … a long time to get the Queen's melidrop.'

'Yes,' said the woman politely.

'Yes!' roared Sir Hugh, as if he just happened to over-hear Sir James' remark. 'But it's only the *Queen* who's waiting. After all, it's only the Queen. Why should *that* fellow hurry?'

The ladies and gentlemen shook their heads in disap-proval, carefully balancing their cups and saucers to avoid spilling their tea.

Sir Hugh shook his head as well, sternly and dramat-ically, so that the gesture could be seen from a distance. The Queen was already watching him.

'Perhaps he's taken a holiday along the way,' Sir Hugh continued scornfully, bellowing as loudly as he could. 'Gone to see the sights! Set off to explore! Gone to visit his mother! Who knows? After all, it's only the Queen who's waiting. And who is a Queen to interfere with the plans of a traveller as great as *Mr Bartlett*?'

Sir Hugh stole another glance at the Queen. He could barely keep himself from smirking. She had suddenly left her group, and was moving towards him. She came like a breeze blowing across the palace park, and the ladies and gentlemen around her, curtsying and bowing, dipped like bright flowers and tall grasses swaying before the wind.

Sir Hugh looked away, so that he could turn back in surprise as the Queen arrived. Then he bowed deeper than anyone else, and gallantly kissed her long white glove.

'Please continue, Sir Hugh,' said the Queen. 'I am sure that what you have been saying is quite fascinating, as usual.'

Sir Hugh smiled bashfully. 'No, Madam. We were merely speculating where Mr Bartlett has got to. I considered that he has gone on a holiday. But Sir James suggested that he has gone diving for oysters off an island.'

'Sir James, really!' said the Queen.

Sir James stared rigidly at the Queen, too frightened to say a word. What would she think?

The Queen smiled.

Sir James grinned in relief. Sir Hugh laughed. Everyone else tittered politely.

The Queen turned back to Sir Hugh. 'And what do you suggest that we ought to do, Sir Hugh, if Mr Bartlett *has* gone on a holiday?'

'Well, we must wait, Madam. Isn't that so? We must *wait* until Mr Bartlett decides that it is time to come back from his holiday. And then, perhaps, Madam may send somebody who will actually go and get a melidrop for her.'

'And who,' said the Queen very quietly, 'will that be?'

'Yes, who?' someone shouted, very loudly. 'Who could it be? We're all dying to know!'

Sir Hugh sighed in exasperation. It was Sutton Pufrock, who had been put in a chair for the garden party and was being carried around by a pair of footmen.

'Never you mind, Sutton Pufrock,' Sir Hugh Lough retorted, flushing with anger. 'We don't need old men poking their noses in if they can't get up and do the job themselves.'

'I can do the job as well as any young upstart who could do with having his bottom spanked,' Sutton Pufrock spluttered, waving his walking-stick and struggling unsuccessfully to get out of his chair.

'Calm down, Pufrock,' Sir Hugh said coldly, 'you'll give yourself a stroke. The Queen knows who can do the job just as well as I do. But let's wait for Bartlett. By all means. How many weeks is it since he left. Twelve? Thirteen? Is it fourteen? Fourteen? Well, fourteen

111

weeks already. And still no news. But there's no rush, is there? After all, it's only the *Queen* who's waiting.'

'Hughie Lough, if I were ten years younger—'

'Well, you're not, are you? So be quiet. Go back to your bed.' Sir Hugh laughed harshly. Sir James laughed as well.

The Queen was gazing at Sir Hugh. 'But you still have not told me what I should do, Sir Hugh.'

'Madam, give me the word. Give me the word, and I will go. Today, I will leave before the sun has set,' Sir Hugh cried, raising his arm dashingly towards the sky. 'Forget Bartlett. You told him you might send me. *Send me!* I beg you.'

'And how will you travel, Sir Hugh?'

'For you, Madam, I would travel through the air. Merely the knowledge that you are waiting would give me wings to fly.'

'And how will you bring the melidrop, Sir Hugh?'

'In a golden casket, Madam. On a bed of velvet.' Sir Hugh dropped to his knee. 'Madam,' he vowed, 'I will bring it back in my heart. My love for you will preserve it.'

The ladies around Sir Hugh sighed. The men applauded.

The Queen gazed at Sir Hugh. Tears came to her eyes.

'Arise, Sir Hugh,' she whispered.

'No, Madam,' said Sir Hugh, bowing his head. 'Give me the word. I will not rise until you send me.'

'Better get a cushion for his knee,' Sutton Pufrock shouted. 'He's going to be there for another three months.'

The Queen stared at Sir Hugh's bowed head.

'Send me, Madam,' implored Sir Hugh. 'Give me the word.'

The Queen's voice was choked. The words to send Sir Hugh were almost on her lips. She looked up for a moment, trying to clear the tears from her eyes. By chance, her glance fell upon Lord Ronald of Tull, who was standing with the Prime Minister and some other politicians. Lord Ronald had not heard a word, but had observed everything and could guess exactly what happening.

Sir Hugh was still kneeling on the ground, arm raised, waiting.

The Queen could not tear her eyes away from her old adviser. Silently, Lord Ronald shook his head.

Chapter 14

THE *Fortune Bey* towed its captive, dragging it through the dark blue water of the ocean. The turbaned figure at the front of the ship pointed the way, and the iceberg followed silently, like a wild beast of the seas that had been hunted and caught. A swathe of foam trailed behind, marking its journey.

Captain Wrick sailed skillfully, as careful and as cautious as a trainer learning to tame a jungle cat. The iceberg followed with docility. When they arrived, Captain Wrick made anchor outside the harbour. He didn't dare to sail closer to the quay, where a gust of wind might have sent the iceberg smashing into other ships. But already a crowd was gathering by the dock. People had never seen such a thing. Workers dropped their crates to stand and stare, pens slipped out of merchants' fingers. What was this huge white rock? Why did it float? Soon every boat in the harbour had taken to the water, oars splashing, crammed to the brim with excited onlookers, and it wasn't long before the fastest of them had reached the iceberg and were circling it with curiosity.

One of the boats edged right up to the ice. As everyone watched, a man in the boat stood up, raised a leg over the side, and rested his foot on it. He put his other foot on the ice. He stood. For a moment he looked down at his own feet, as if he could not believe what he was doing. Then he straightened up, looked around, and gave a mighty yell. Everyone yelled back. He tried to take a step and fell flat on his face. Five minutes later the iceberg was covered with people crawling, falling, slithering and sliding. Then the first hammers and chisels arrived, and people were chipping pieces of ice to take back to their families as souvenirs.

This was too much! In these warm waters, the iceberg would soon be melting fast. All it needed was a crowd of people knocking blocks off to make it disappear altogether. Together with the five biggest members of Captain Wrick's crew, Jacques le Grand went to clear everyone off the ice. In the meantime, Bartlett went ashore to look for Gozo. On the way he passed the town's scholar, who was being rowed out to look at the iceberg. He was wearing his floppy hat and carried three big books under his arm. They must have rushed him straight from the library. The scholar did not look comfortable. He looked nervous and bewildered. He was gripping the sides of his boat with whitened knuckles. The scholar looked as if he preferred to learn about the world from the books in his peaceful library than by sitting in a damp, rocking boat with his feet tangled up in nets that smelled of fish.

But where was Gozo? The quay was still filling up as news of the iceberg spread through the town. Mothers were arriving with their children, old people were waving their walking-sticks to get to the front. Crowds of people jostled and pushed, trying to get onto a boat that would take them to see the dazzling white rock that floated in the distance. Yet Gozo was nowhere to be seen.

Bartlett went to the bazaar. With everyone at the port, the streets of the town were strangely empty and silent. Now and again someone ran past him. Their footsteps echoed.

In the bazaar the traders were still standing by their stalls, wondering what had happened to all the people who should have been milling around. Bartlett found the old melidrop-seller who had told him about Gozo months earlier. He was wearing the same cotton cap, sitting on his backless chair and staring glumly at all the melidrops piled up on his stall, for which there was not a single customer.

Bartlett called out to him.

The old man looked up with a start. He jumped to his feet and began shovelling melidrops into a sack. 'Two bags, three bags for the gentleman?' he cried.

'I don't want any melidrops,' said Bartlett.

'Half price, half price for the gentleman.'

'None for me.'

'Quarter price. Quarter price.'

'No. None.'

'What do you want me to do, *pay* you to take them?' the old man demanded angrily. He held the sack upside down and emptied the melidrops onto his stall.

The old man sat down again. He peered at Bartlett.

'I remember you,' he said suddenly, wiggling a finger disapprovingly. 'You didn't want any melidrops last time, either. They shouldn't let people like you into the bazaar. You set a bad example. Look around you. Where is everybody? It's like a ghost-town. Off they all ran, shouting about some rock floating in the sea. Rocks floating in their heads, if you ask me. And what do we get in return? The man who doesn't buy anything!'

Bartlett grinned. 'Where's Gozo?'

'How should I know?' The old man waved a hand in disgust.

'Was he here today?'

'Look at my stall. Do you think these melidrops walked here? He's probably asleep where he always is. Or looking for the floating rock, like everybody else,' the

118

old man called after him, as Bartlett set off for the well outside the city gate.

Gozo was in the back of his wagon with his hat over his face, exactly as he had been the first time Bartlett found him. Only the wagon drivers, who had already gone to sleep, had not heard about the iceberg. Bartlett quietly lifted the hat off Gozo's face. Gozo opened his eyes and blinked sleepily. Then he recognised Bartlett and sat bolt upright, grinning from ear to ear.

'Mr Bartlett, you've come back!'

'Yes.'

'And have you brought the ice-rock?'

'Iceberg. Of course, I said I would.'

'Where is it?' Gozo looked around excitedly, as if Bartlett was supposed to have brought it to the well.

The drivers in the other wagons were starting to sit up, looking curiously at the man talking to Gozo.

'We haven't got time to see it now,' said Bartlett.

'When will we see it?' asked Gozo anxiously.

'Later.'

'It might be gone later.'

'It won't be gone. Not without me, that's for sure. Now, come on, get up. We've got to get going.'

'Where?'

'To Mordi's farm. We need a melidrop. The freshest and plumpest we can find.'

Chapter 15

EVERYONE WAS STILL asleep at Mordi's farm when they arrived. There was no rush to get up. It was Monday, and the bazaar would be closed tomorrow, so they would not be harvesting that night.

Gozo unharnessed the horses and took them into the stable. Bartlett walked over to the well. He looked down into its dark depths. Then he tossed the bucket in and heard it land with a splash. He hauled it up and tasted the pure, icy water that kept Mordi's melidrops fresh and made them the best in the bazaar.

'Good and cold, eh?' said Mordi, who must have been woken up by the sound of the wagon, and was now standing in the doorway of the house, wearing only his trousers. He laughed his big, booming laugh and scratched his belly. 'So you're back, Bartlett?'

Bartlett nodded, grinning.

'They've got the ice-rock, Uncle Mo!' shouted Gozo, poking his head round the stable doorway.

'The ice-rock! Have you seen it, Gozo?'

'No, but I will.'

'When?'

'Tomorrow,' said Bartlett.

'Tomorrow!' shouted Gozo, disappearing into the stable again.

Mordi came over to the well. He hauled up a bucket and emptied it over his head, doing his cold water dance and shouting 'I love it, *I love it!*' as the water ran down his back. Bartlett watched him with a grin.

'That boy,' said Mordi eventually, giving one last shiver and shake, 'hasn't stopped talking about the ice-rock since you left. Not a day goes by when he doesn't say: 'Do you think Mr Bartlett will be back today with the ice-rock?' Every day he says it, before he goes to the bazaar.'

'Iceberg, Mordi. It's called an iceberg.'

Mordi shrugged. 'Is there really such a thing? I know what you explorers are like, Bartlett, always telling stories. Each mountain you climb is bigger than the last. The boy will be disappointed if you've been making fun of him. He won't just be disappointed, he'll be crushed. I don't know what I'll say to him.'

'I haven't been making fun of him,' said Bartlett. 'The iceberg's there all right, floating in the harbour. Gozo will see it tomorrow.'

'He wants to be a traveller now. He wants to be an explorer. Every day, before he goes to the bazaar, he says: "I wish I was an explorer like Mr Bartlett."'

'I thought he asks about the iceberg.'

'*After* he asks about the iceberg.' Mordi smiled. 'So,

121

Bartlett, it's nice to see you back safe again. But what can we do for you here on the farm? Shouldn't you be off to see the Queen.'

'He's come for a melidrop, Uncle Mo,' shouted Gozo, tearing out of the stable.

'Couldn't you get one at the bazaar?'

Bartlett shook his head. Nothing but the freshest melidrop from Mordi's orchard would do.

Before sunset, Bartlett, Gozo and Mordi went into the orchard. It was the end of the season, but there were still some remarkable fruit, splashes of red and gold, hanging amongst the dark leaves of the melidrop trees. Mordi glanced left and right as they walked, pointing out melidrops that looked especially promising and making a note in his mind of the trees on which they hung. He knew each tree in his orchard as if it were a person.

'What does the Queen want?' he inquired. 'Taste, perfume, texture, colour?' He stopped and pointed to a plump orange melidrop hanging high in a tree. 'Now, that's a melidrop you would want for its perfume. Its taste would have medium sweetness, but its scent would be powerful and long-lasting.'

Bartlett stared at the orange melidrop. It was like a spot of bright, flaming paint dabbed on the dark leaves.

'Now, what is it that you want?' said Mordi.

Bartlett considered. Perfume? Colour? Taste? He had

never thought about it before. A melidrop was a melidrop.

Mordi glanced at Gozo. 'They just don't understand melidrops over there' he murmured, shaking his head, and Gozo shook his head as well.

'Taste,' said Bartlett. 'If it has to be something, it's taste.'

'Are you sure?'

Bartlett nodded.

'All right,' said Mordi, 'taste it is.'

Now Mordi began to walk faster, with a frown of concentration as he peered from side to side. 'Taste … taste,' he muttered. 'Strong and spicy or creamy and sweet? Sweetly spiced? Strongly creamed?' Half an hour later he was still leading them through the orchard, peering around and muttering, occasionally stroking his beard in thought.

Bartlett was beginning to wonder if it really were so important. After all, the Queen had never eaten a melidrop before. She wasn't an expert. How would she know if she were eating a special one or an ordinary one?

Suddenly Mordi stopped. 'We've seen enough.'

Bartlett agreed. They were deep in the orchard. He had lost track of where they were.

'It's that yellow one, isn't it, Uncle Mo?' demanded Gozo, pointing excitedly to a large melidrop hanging on a tree not far from where they had stopped.

'Not bad, Gozo,' said Mordi. 'That would have been my second choice. But my first choice is back at the place where Grandma Zole broke her leg.'

Gozo wrinkled his nose. 'I can't remember a good one there.'

'You weren't looking hard enough,' said Mordi, and he set off back through the trees, with Bartlett and Gozo following.

Now Mordi did not look around, as if he did not want to be distracted once he had made his decision. He led them rapidly through the orchard. Five minutes later he stopped.

'Is this the place where Grandma Zole broke her leg?' asked Bartlett.

'Just over there, she tripped over that root,' said Mordi.

Bartlett felt sorry for Grandma Zole.

'She's dead now,' said Gozo. 'Where's the melidrop, Uncle Mo?'

'Can't you see it?'

Gozo looked around. Mordi watched him keenly. Gozo's face was growing more and more perplexed.

'I don't know,' Gozo said eventually.

'Can't guess?'

Gozo shook his head.

Mordi took a step towards the tree closest to Bartlett.

Triumphantly, he swept aside a branch. There, just three feet off the ground, hung a red melidrop. Mordi must have caught no more than a glimpse of it when they walked past earlier.

Gozo frowned. 'I didn't see it, Uncle Mo.'

Bartlett took a step closer and peered at the melidrop. It wasn't the biggest one he had seen. There were narrow yellow streaks on its red skin, and a tiny wrinkle as well. Bartlett wasn't impressed. After all the melidrops

they had seen, was this the one that was fit for a Queen?

Mordi saw the look on Bartlett's face and he threw his head back, filling the orchard with his booming laughter. 'Taste, Bartlett. That's what you wanted. If it's looks you want, we'll get you another. But if it's taste—if it's flavour—this is the one. It will taste ... like spiced currants dipped in sweet wine and rolled in date powder ...'

'And creamy,' added Gozo.

'Yes ... as if it were mixed with honey and made into a custard with a touch of vanilla and a hint of rosewater.'

Bartlett stared at the melidrop doubtfully. How could one little fruit have so many flavours?

'This is the one, Bartlett. Trust me. I wouldn't even send it to the bazaar. This one, I would give to Vara.'

Bartlett glanced at Mordi. Then he reached out for the melidrop.

Mordi grabbed Bartlett's arm before he could touch it.

'Not now,' he said. 'At dawn, when the air is coolest, when the water is coldest. That's the time to pick it.'

Chapter 16

THEY PICKED THE Queen's melidrop at dawn. Mordi, carrying a lantern, led the whole family through the darkness of the orchard to the place where Grandma Zole broke her leg. He pulled back the branch to reveal the red melidrop with yellow streaks.

'Bartlett is going to take this melidrop to the Queen' he said.

Everyone stared solemnly at the melidrop. They all knew that Bartlett was taking it to the Queen, but somehow Mordi's statement seemed to give the melidrop even more importance.

Mordi handed his lantern to Vara. The deep shadows of the trees danced as the flame wavered. Mordi pulled a thin silver knife from a scabbard that was attached to his belt and crouched under a branch. Now his hands were in darkness behind the leaves and no one could see what he was doing. Suddenly he gave a single sharp, sure flick of the wrist. When he stood up again he was holding the melidrop.

They carried it straight back to the yard and plunged it into a bucket of cold, freshly drawn water. Gozo's horses were already hitched to the wagon and ready to go. Gozo jumped up. Bartlett climbed aboard and Mordi joined them, carrying the bucket with the melidrop. Everyone else piled into the back. No one wanted to miss out on seeing the iceberg. Even the three men who worked for Mordi during the harvest were coming along.

The bazaar was closed for the day and the road should have been empty, but a long column of carts and wagons stretched in front of them. News of the iceberg had obviously spread. All the way Gozo asked questions about the iceberg. How had they captured it? How had they brought it back? He wanted to know everything. He wanted to know about other trips Bartlett had made. He wanted to know where the Queen lived and how Bartlett and Jacques le Grand were going to get there. He wanted to know how Bartlett had become an explorer. Bartlett chuckled and answered each of Gozo's questions. Finally Gozo looked at him hesitantly and asked whether Bartlett thought it would be possible for someone like him, Gozo, to be an explorer as well.

Bartlett smiled. Yes, he said, he thought it would be possible for someone like Gozo to be an explorer.

Gozo drove straight to the quay when they arrived at the town. As they came around the corner and caught their first sight of the iceberg, everybody gasped. Gozo stopped the horses and stared. Everyone in the back stared as well. They stood up and stared some more. In the distance, the iceberg floated placidly behind the three masts of the *Fortune Bey*. Under the bright morning sun it was so white, clean, pure, its jagged outline looked so crisp, it was like something that had come from a different world.

There was already a crowd at the waterfront. Even the scholar had returned, but this time he was staying on dry land. He sat on a folding stool at the edge of the quay, balancing a big pad of paper on his knees and sketching the iceberg. On his left there was a man holding an umbrella to protect him from the sun, and on his right someone else was holding a tray of breakfast delicacies.

Bartlett found a boat to take him out to the *Fortune Bey*. Gozo and Mordi went with him. Mordi refused to let go of the bucket until the Queen's melidrop was safely stored, and Gozo wouldn't be satisfied unless he could set foot on the ice himself. He wanted to see the *Fortune Bey* as well. Jacques le Grand was waiting on the ship. He welcomed Bartlett with an unusually grumpy expression on his face. He had spent the whole of the previous day chasing souvenir hunters off the iceberg, and no sooner had he left it at night than a swarm of shadowy figures returned and the *click-click-click* of chisels was heard once more. So back Jacques went. He had spent the whole night on the ice without a wink of sleep, and had left it only an hour before.

'Well, Jacques,' said Bartlett, nodding towards the iceberg, 'it's time to go back!'

While Bartlett had been away, Captain Wrick had sent Michael to find a large drill in the town. It was like a gigantic corkscrew, six feet long and with a tip of iron. They took it with them in the boat. As soon as they drew up beside the ice Gozo leapt out. He jumped on it with all his weight and couldn't believe that it was really made of water. Bartlett, Jacques and Mordi got out onto

the ice as well, watched by the people circling in boats. At first Mordi was very tentative. After all, if Bartlett were to be believed, he was standing on water! What was to stop it becoming liquid again? Only after a long time was he confident enough to put down the bucket with the melidrop, and even then he continued to stand alongside it, just in case it started to sink.

By this time Bartlett had punched a hole in the ice with a hammer. Then he and Jacques took hold of the drill. They pointed it into the hole and worked opposite one another to turn it. The ice was hard and they had to strain with all the strength of their arms and push down with all the weight of their bodies to drive it in. Slowly the drill ground down into the ice, churning up a mound of glistening slivers as it bored deeper and deeper.

The drill went down five feet and made a hole as wide as a fist. When it was finished, Mordi took the melidrop out of the bucket. He raised it and paused to take one last good look. The water from the dripping melidrop ran down his arm.

'I hope the Queen enjoys it,' he said. He spoke as if the melidrop were almost too precious to let go.

'She will,' said Bartlett. 'Come on, Mordi, it's only a fruit. We haven't got all day. If we don't get it frozen soon it won't be any good.'

Mordi crouched beside the hole with the melidrop in his hand. He put his arm in as far as it would go. When his arm came out, his hand was empty. The melidrop was gone.

Bartlett peered into the hole. He could just glimpse a hint of red in the depths. He pushed back the slivers of ice. Now the melidrop could not be seen at all.

They went back to the *Fortune Bey*. Jacques took the tools and climbed back up the rope ladder. Bartlett turned to say goodbye to Gozo and Mordi, but suddenly Gozo leapt onto the ladder, scampered up the side of the ship and disappeared over the ship's rail. A moment later his face looked down at them.

'I'm not going back, Uncle Mo!' he shouted.

'What do you mean?' demanded Mordi. He had jumped to his feet and the boat rocked as his voice thundered.

'I'm not going back!' shouted Gozo. 'I'm going with Bartlett. I'm going to see the Queen.'

Mordi turned angrily to Bartlett. 'What have you been saying to him?'

'Nothing.' Bartlett was as surprised as Mordi.

'What have you promised him?'

'Nothing. You said yourself he wanted to be a traveller.'

'I didn't say he *could* be a traveller! What will I tell his mother? *Excuse me, Gozo went on a journey with a fruit and a rock made out of water.* Bartlett, I'm meant to look after him! That's why his mother lets him drive for me during the harvest.' Mordi looked up at the ship again. 'Come down now, Gozo. Come down this instant!'

'No!' shouted Gozo, 'I'm going with Bartlett.'

Mordi sat down with his head in his hands. 'I thought this might happen,' he mumbled. 'I told Vara last night, we shouldn't let him come today. I told her. But she said the boy would never forgive us if we didn't let him see the iceberg. She said we would just have to keep an eye on him.'

Other faces were appearing over the ship's rail to see what was going to happen. Soon the whole crew was looking down at the boat, where Mordi was shaking his head anxiously.

'I should go and get Vara,' he muttered, glancing towards the shore with a worried look. 'Vara would know how to get him down.' Mordi jumped to his feet again. 'What about the wagon?' he shouted. 'Who's going to drive it?'

'Selig,' shouted Gozo, 'he wants to drive it.'

'Selig harvests. That's what Selig does.'

'You can spare him. The harvest's almost over.'

Mordi shook his head despairingly again. 'And what about next season?' he shouted suddenly. 'What about next season?'

'I'll be back next season,' shouted Gozo. 'I'm only going to see the Queen.'

Mordi looked at Bartlett. 'Will he be back?' he asked quietly.

Bartlett shrugged. Gozo was peering down at them with a frown, straining to hear what they were saying. 'If he wants to,' said Bartlett.

Mordi sighed. 'All right,' he shouted. 'All right, Gozo, but—'

Mordi couldn't be heard. Captain Wrick's men were cheering. 'Good for you, Uncle Mo!' one of them shouted. Even Mordi grinned at that. But the grin didn't last long.

'I don't know what I'm going to say to his mother,' he muttered. 'Maybe I should go up and get him! Maybe I should just go up there and grab him!'

'You'll have to catch him first,' said Bartlett.

'Maybe I should go and get Vara. *Vara* would get him down.'

'Is she faster than you?'

'No, but she's a lot more frightening when she wants to be.'

Bartlett laughed.

'You'd better tell your captain to get going as soon as I leave,' said Mordi with a sigh, 'because Vara will be after him the second she finds out. She's never been near a boat before, but that won't stop her. And if she catches *you*, I hate to think what she'll do!'

Bartlett grinned.

'Will you look after him, Bartlett?' Mordi said, looking at him seriously.

'Of course.'

'Properly? I have to be able to tell his mother.'

'Properly,' said Bartlett.

Mordi nodded. 'How long will it take you to get to the Queen?'

'Nine weeks, Mordi. A bit more or a bit less, depending on the winds.'

'Nine weeks! That's an awfully long time to be on a ship.'

'Not so long,' said Bartlett.

'Gozo's never been on a ship before, you know.'

'No one's ever been on a ship before they've been on one,' said Bartlett.

'No, I suppose not. But it's a long time. The Queen must be a very patient person. How long is it since you left her?'

'Four or five months,' said Bartlett, who hadn't been counting.

'Well, I suppose she'll be happy to see you after all this time.'

Bartlett grinned. 'I'm sure she will.'

'All right, Bartlett. All right,' said Mordi, shaking his head. 'Just don't let him say anything silly to the Queen. Gozo's quite excitable, you know.'

Bartlett laughed. He put a foot on the rope-ladder and hoisted himself up. The boatman pushed away from the side of the ship.

'Mordi,' called Bartlett, swinging from the rope-ladder.

'What?'

'Thanks for the melidrop.'

Mordi nodded. For a second his face was still serious.

Then he grinned. He began to laugh. The sound boomed out of his beard. It rolled across the water, bounced against the ship, streamed up the side and flooded over the deck, echoing in Bartlett's ears as he climbed aboard.

Captain Wrick was already at the wheel. The men were already unfurling the sails. The anchor came up. Even before Mordi reached shore, the *Fortune Bey* turned and headed out to sea, taking the magical, impossible rock of ice with it.

Chapter 17

AFTER THE GARDEN party, Lord Ronald of Tull didn't have tea with the Queen for weeks. One Thursday she sent word that she was unwell, and told him to stay home. The next week she sent word that the Chancellor of the University was very upset about the way the students were behaving and wanted to see her at once. One week she didn't send word at all, and Lord Ronald arrived at the palace only to find that she was out riding. The next day she sent to say that she had forgotten. *Forgotten!* They had been having tea together on Thursday afternoons for years. If the Queen had forgotten about tea on Thursday afternoons she would be forgetting that she was a Queen next. Already she was behaving not exactly as a Queen ought.

But this week the Queen did not send a footman with an excuse, and she was not out riding, and nothing else out of the ordinary had happened. Lord Ronald found himself sitting in the familiar panelled room with the table and the crisp white tablecloth. The Queen poured the tea as usual. Everything seemed to be just as it always was. But everything was not as it always was, and Lord Ronald could see it at once.

'It's only the *Queen* who's waiting,' the Queen said eventually. 'That's what people are saying, Lord Ronald. I know it is hard to believe that people could say this, but I am told that it is true. Lord Ronald, this cannot be good, for people to be saying such things. If this is what they are saying now, heaven knows what they will be saying next.'

'That the Queen is patient?' said Lord Ronald, reaching for a cake. He stared. There were lemon slices on the plate! Where were the butter cakes? What had the Queen done with the butter cakes?

'Is something wrong, Lord Ronald?' asked the Queen.

'No, Madam,' said Lord Ronald. 'I was merely surprised. I thought there would be butter cakes.'

'Ah. Well, if you want butter cakes, Lord Ronald, you will have to wait. I'm sorry. Perhaps next week. Or the week after. Or perhaps in *seven months*.'

Lord Ronald nodded. He even smiled. He hated lemon slices. He had always hated lemon slices. He hated lemons, and putting them in slices didn't make them any better.

'Very nice, Madam,' he said, taking a bite and wincing at the taste. He put the rest of the cake down on his plate.

It was the bitterest lemon slice he had ever eaten.

'Yes, I like them,' said the Queen, taking a tiny nibble of one.

'Madam, waiting is never easy—'

'I can wait, Lord Ronald. Seven months?' the Queen laughed unconvincingly. 'Of course I can wait! But what if they come back with nothing at the end of it. What then?'

'That would be difficult, I admit.'

'Difficult? Difficult? No, difficult is not the word. Impossible. No, not impossible. *Intolerable!* And horrible. Yes, horrible and intolerable—those are the words.'

'And insufferable?'

'Insufferable. Yes. That's another good word. A very good word, Lord Ronald. It *would* be insufferable. But not for my sake, Lord Ronald. Goodness, no. I'm only thinking of my people. What will they think, if they see their Queen waiting for seven months—for nothing? They would be disappointed, distraught...'

'Devastated?'

'Yes, devastated. That's a good word for it. That is exactly what they would be. Devastated. I cannot let that happen to my people.'

'Of course not,' said Lord Ronald, wondering if even the Queen herself believed what she was saying. 'But what do you want to do, Madam?'

The Queen did not reply. She glanced hesitantly at Lord Ronald.

'Madam, do you want to know what I think?'

'Lord Ronald,' said the Queen, who could tell when he was getting into the mood to make one of his fiery speeches, 'I don't think that is the right tone—'

'I think it is Sir Hugh Lough who has been putting these thoughts into your head.'

'Lord Ronald!'

'He disliked Bartlett from the very moment he saw him. He cannot bear anyone else to outshine him. *He* wouldn't know how to get you a raspberry, much less a melidrop. But send someone else to get it and he will do anything he can to prevent it.'

'Is that what you think, Lord Ronald?'

'It is!' Nothing could stop Lord Ronald now. 'And what about all that nonsense at the garden party? Throwing his arm around! On his knees! I believe he is still there waiting for *the word*.'

'Of course he isn't! Do you think I would let the poor man stay there in the rain and the wind?'

'No, Madam. It's just as well! He would only be in the way if he were allowed to stay there.'

'He would not be in the way,' the Queen said impatiently. Suddenly she became curious. 'Whose way do you think he would be in?'

'The rhinoceros' way.'

The Queen thought for a moment. 'True. He might be in the rhinoceros' way.'

'Or the water buffalo's.'

'No. He was nowhere near the water buffalo. They always stay by the lake.'

Lord Ronald shook his head. 'I hear that Sir Hugh intends to travel through the air and bring you a melidrop in his heart.'

'There is nothing Sir Hugh would not do for me, Lord Ronald,' the Queen informed him in her sternest tone. 'It would not hurt if others occasionally recalled their duty to their Queen.'

'Then send him, Madam, at once. By all means. I have not seen a man fly for a long time.'

The Queen stared at Lord Ronald icily.

'And as for melidrops in a heart,' said Lord Ronald, 'I doubt that has been done since the world began.'

The Queen picked up the plate of cakes. 'Do have another lemon slice, Lord Ronald.'

'No, thank you. One is quite enough, and I have not completely finished it yet.'

'*Do* have another,' said the Queen, almost pushing the plate into Lord Ronald's chest, 'you always eat at least four butter cakes.'

Lord Ronald reluctantly took a lemon slice.

'Now eat it, Lord Ronald.'

'Madam . . .'

'Eat!'

Lord Ronald ate. There were tears in his eyes. The

Queen watched him until the last bitter morsel had been swallowed.

Lord Ronald gulped a mouthful of tea. He gulped another, and another, until the taste of the lemon slice had gone.

Suddenly the Queen laughed mischievously. 'Oh, Lord Ronald. I can see that you too would do anything for me.'

'Almost anything, Madam,' he replied hoarsely. 'If you want someone to eat another lemon slice, you had better call Sir Hugh.'

'They aren't very nice, are they?'

'No. They are not.'

'I made them myself, you know.'

'I am very sorry to hear it.' Lord Ronald reached for the teapot and poured himself another cup of tea. He became serious once more. 'Madam, you know that you cannot send Sir Hugh.'

'Why not? I said that I would send him if Bartlett did

not bring back a melidrop, and Bartlett has *not* brought back a melidrop.'

'But he told you it might take seven months. And it is only five months.'

'And how do I know that he is even trying? How do I know he hasn't gone to an island to dive for oysters.'

Lord Ronald shook his head. 'Oysters? Only Sir Hugh could think of that.'

The Queen shrugged. 'Besides, Sir Hugh does not demand anything. Bartlett *demands* an expedition to . . . those caverns. Is that the way to speak to a Queen, making demands? Sir Hugh, of course, asks for nothing.'

'Sir Hugh will *do* nothing. Besides, Madam, Bartlett did not demand. *You* offered.'

'Lord Ronald, I don't think that has—'

'*You* made a deal.'

'Lord Ronald!' cried the Queen, and she looked as if she were going to force him to eat another lemon slice.

'Well, it's true, Madam.'

'Well, if it *is* true, Lord Ronald, it is also true that I said I would not give him an expedition if I sent Sir Hugh. And I did not say when I might send him.'

'But Bartlett told you it might take seven—'

'I did not say *when* I might send him!' the Queen repeated sharply.

The Queen and Lord Ronald stared at one another, each breathing heavily.

'Madam,' Lord Ronald said softly, 'the whole country knows that you were told it might take seven months. Your people expect you to wait. If you think Sir Hugh is doing you a favour by asking to be sent, you are mistaken. Greatly mistaken. If you send him now, you will seem too impatient. Ask yourself what your people will be saying about you *then*.'

The Queen tapped her fingers, very fast, considering. Her rings flashed in Lord Ronald's eyes.

'Madam, Sir Hugh has not forgiven Bartlett for his insult.'

'And he should not have insulted him!'

'True. But in his revenge against Bartlett, he is using you.'

'Me? The Queen? He cannot use a Queen!'

Lord Ronald raised an eyebrow. 'No? Do not be too sure. There is no one who cannot be used. Each of us has a weakness that can be exploited by others. Your father, the King, used to say that himself.'

'Lord Ronald, are you saying—'

'Impatient, Madam?' Lord Ronald glanced at the footman beside the door. The footman looked away suddenly, as if he had not been listening. 'Am I saying that you are sometimes just a *tiny* bit too impatient? Am I saying that this is something which others may use for their own purposes? Madam, you amaze me. You have worked it all out for yourself!'

The Queen narrowed her eyes, gazing at Lord Ronald. There was no one quite like Lord Ronald to find a way of saying what he chose, even when one didn't want to hear it.

'Madam,' said Lord Ronald softly, 'do not send him within the seven months.'

'It is two months more to wait!'

'It is *only* two months more. Much less than you have already waited.'

The Queen considered. Her rings flashed.

'Wait, Madam. For your people's sake.'

The Queen frowned. Eventually she sighed. 'All right, Lord Ronald. I will wait two months more—but not a day longer. When the seven months are up, on that very morning, at the exact time that Bartlett left, I will send Sir Hugh. And if they have not brought me a melidrop by then, Bartlett and his friend will get *nothing* for their expedition.'

Chapter 18

ONCE MORE THE *Fortune Bey* was far from land. It plunged through the waves, leading the iceberg across the ocean. By now Captain Wrick had learned all the skills of an iceberg-tower: he could tell how the ice would move when the ship sailed into a fresh current or when the wind changed direction and picked up speed, how it would pitch when the waves rose or a storm appeared on the horizon. Sometimes he let out the chains and allowed more slack for the iceberg to float further away, and at other times he ordered his men to wind the chains in until it trailed close behind. He began to feel as if he had been towing icebergs all his life.

But for Bartlett, this part of the journey was not the same as before. Before, it had been an adventure, wondering how they could get a melidrop, then whether they could capture an iceberg, then whether they could tow it. Perhaps he had not really believed that it could be done. But now, they *did* have an iceberg, and they *were* towing it, and there *was* a melidrop inside it. The difficulties had been overcome, the adventurous part was over. Yet there was still a whole ocean to be crossed before the melidrop could be delivered.

One day, when they had already been sailing for two weeks, another ship appeared in the distance. It changed course and came closer. Suddenly a row of coloured flags appeared amongst its sails. Captain Wrick put his telescope to his eye. He muttered an order to Michael, and a moment later a row of flags answered from the mast of the *Fortune Bey*.

'What's happening?' asked Bartlett.

'The other captain's coming aboard.' Captain Wrick laughed. 'He would like to drink the Queen's health. He says that he will bring the whisky if I supply the ice!'

Two of Captain Wrick's men rowed out to the iceberg and cut a bucket full of ice-cubes, which were put into the excellent whisky that Captain Trobottam, the captain from the other ship, brought with him. Captain

Wrick, Michael, Captain Trobottam, Bartlett and Jacques le Grand solemnly raised their glasses to the Queen's health and settled back in their chairs in Captain Wrick's cabin to enjoy their whisky. Even Gozo had a glass, although he coughed and spluttered each time he swallowed. Everybody was enjoying the occasion immensely and obviously thought they were extremely clever to have found a way of drinking whisky and ice at sea. Only Bartlett felt ill at ease, and kept glancing at Jacques le Grand who was shovelling another load of ice-cubes into his glass and pouring himself seconds. It wasn't the whisky that Bartlett was worried about. It was the ice.

The iceberg was melting. Really melting.

Of course everyone knew that the ice was *going* to melt, and everyone knew that it had started to melt even before they had stopped to pick up the melidrop, but somehow back then the iceberg was still so big that it just wasn't possible to imagine it melting away to nothing. But now you could see the difference day by day. Each day the jagged edges of the iceberg looked a little smoother, it became a little smaller, and the smaller it became the more quickly it appeared to diminish.

A couple of weeks later Bartlett woke up in a cold sweat. He had just had a terrible dream: the iceberg had broken up into five little pieces and each of the pieces was floating off by itself and melting away five times as fast as the single block would have done. He rushed up on deck. The iceberg was still there in one piece, drifting behind the ship and gleaming in the moonlight. But what would happen if it really did break up? And how quickly would it melt even if it stayed in one piece? They were still not even halfway across the ocean. Even if the winds were favourable, there were still another four weeks of sailing to go. Who could tell if the iceberg would last?

Captain Wrick, of course, thought he could. Smoking his pipe, he made all sorts of calculations and came up with a different answer every day. Half the time he was sure the iceberg would make it—the rest of the time he was sure it wouldn't. The day he agreed to chop ice-cubes for Captain Trobottam was one of the days when he thought it would. The next morning he emerged from his cabin and apologised to Bartlett. There were new calculations! He had forgotten to take into account the fact that seabirds sometimes landed on the iceberg, warming it up with the heat of their bodies. The iceberg, Captain Wrick announced, would therefore melt faster than he had calculated. In fact, there was no hope. No hope, he said. He wished now that he had never given the order to cut ice-cubes from it. But an order cannot be taken back once it has been given, just as whisky is gone once it is drunk. There was no point wishing otherwise. In fact, he said, trying to cheer Bartlett up, if the iceberg wasn't going to make it, it couldn't hurt to chop off a few ice-cubes while they still had the chance!

Bartlett stopped listening to Captain Wrick's predictions. He just asked him to drink his whisky without ice.

They had to drill a new hole for the melidrop because the ice melted so much that it was now only a few inches below the surface. Ten days later it was almost at the surface again. This time, when they drilled, a hunk of ice broke off and floated away. When they tried in a different place, the end of the drill broke through the bottom and the hole filled with water. So they cut some ice and put it in a barrel with the frozen melidrop and took it back on board the *Fortune Bey*.

After that, someone had to row across to the iceberg each day and cut a fresh supply of ice. The ship was making slow progress. Bartlett hardly slept. Ten times a day he went to the back of the ship to look at the iceberg and remind himself how much was left. All night he lay awake in his hammock, wondering how much would remain in the morning. He could hardly bear to think of the magnificent iceberg that they had captured all those long weeks before, when it was big enough to have sunk a ship and large enough for a whole family of seals to roll around on. Now, it could not even hold a melidrop.

It was a question of time. Would the iceberg last long enough? Would the melidrop spoil? It was no longer the expedition to the Margoulis Caverns that made Bartlett want to succeed—he hadn't thought about that for a long time. Getting the melidrop had been a real adventure in itself. Just as Sutton Pufrock had predicted, it had required all the tools of the explorer: Inventiveness, Desperation and Perseverance. But now it was out of his hands. Now there was nothing to do but wait as the *Fortune Bey* made its way across the sea. It was all a question of time. And as the iceberg melted, time was running out.

Chapter 19

NOTHING CAPTAIN WRICK could do could make the *Fortune Bey* go faster. When the wind died down he just had to wait until it picked up again. When the current turned he had to alter course. These were the laws of the sea and no one could change them. In the meantime, the iceberg got smaller and smaller. Two of the harpoons attaching it to the chains fell out. Captain Wrick reeled in the last chain until the iceberg was only a short distance behind the ship. It didn't look big enough now to do any damage, even if it crashed into the hull with all its weight. It didn't look big enough to do much damage to a rowboat. It looked like something that had fallen overboard by mistake.

Captain Wrick didn't say anything. No more calculations, no predictions. He sat in his cabin with his charts, poring over them for hours to find the shortest course back. They were only days away. But days, hours, would make the difference. Not even Captain Wrick could make the winds blow or the currents run.

One morning the sailors came back from the iceberg and said it wasn't possible to cut any more ice out of when it was still in the sea. It was no longer big enough to stand on and every time they hit it with the pick it pitched and heaved in the water. So they reeled in the iceberg and tied ropes around it, and then they hauled it up onto the deck, like some kind of big, dead, glassy fish that they had captured. Gozo looked at it sadly. They chopped it up into blocks, and carried them below deck where it was cool. And then Bartlett or Jacques le Grand chopped the blocks into smaller chunks whenever more ice was needed to keep the melidrop frozen in its bucket.

And then one morning there were only two small blocks left.

They lay on a shelf in a dark room beside the ship's pantry. Streams of water dribbled onto the floor beside the bucket containing the melidrop. It would be the last time that Bartlett replaced its ice. By the end of the day the two small blocks would have melted. And when that had happened, the melidrop itself would start to thaw, first softening, then ripening, then spoiling.

When would they reach land? Bartlett didn't know. No one knew for certain. Today or tomorrow. Maybe the next day. Maybe when the melidrop could still be eaten. Maybe after it had turned into repulsive brown sludge.

Bartlett placed his hands on the cold, wet surface of the ice blocks. For some reason, he was reluctant to lift them. The dark room was very quiet, and Bartlett was alone. His fingers started to go numb, yet he did not raise them. For a long time he gazed vacantly at the last two pale pieces of the iceberg. If the ice melted, if the melidrop thawed and rotted, then everyone would say that they had failed. But hadn't they really succeeded? He and Jacques, together with Gozo, and Captain Wrick, and Mordi, and Michael, and all the others who had helped along the way, had captured an iceberg, and towed it across thousands of miles of ocean, and preserved a melidrop for weeks. No one had done any of these things before. Did it really matter now if the melidrop reached the Queen? It was a question of hours, that was all. How had it happened that these particular hours had suddenly become so important?

Bartlett was so deep in thought that it was a long time before he became aware of the shouting that was coming from the deck.

Everyone had already rushed on deck by the time Bartlett arrived. Captain Wrick was peering through his telescope. Gozo had scampered up the rigging and joined the lookout in the crow's nest.

'Can you see?' said the lookout.

Gozo squinted. 'Where?'

'There. Can't you see? Look.'

Gozo squinted harder. There was a smudge, just a faint smudge, as if someone had smeared a little dirt above the horizon.

'Land,' said the lookout.

Captain Wrick brought the *Fortune Bey* around and steered hard for the harbour. He raised the emergency flag, which is used only when there is an urgent message or a dying man on board, or some other reason that a ship must be allowed to dock without delay, and every other captain must make way for him.

Early in the afternoon they entered the mouth of the

bay, where the water was always choppy. The *Fortune Bey* pitched until it reached the calmer waters of the harbour. Other ships stood by as Captain Wrick passed. Only one ignored the emergency flag. It was heading for the open sea and it slashed straight across their course, forcing the *Bey* to slacken speed. Captain Wrick whipped out his telescope and examined it. His compressed lips showed his anger. Bartlett looked through the telescope as well.

'You know who that is, standing at the bridge on that ship, don't you?' said Bartlett.

Jacques took the telescope and looked. He nodded, grinning.

'Who?' demanded Captain Wrick.

'Sir Hugh Lough,' said Bartlett. 'The Queen's favourite. You'd recognise him anywhere by the way he stands.'

Jacques placed his right foot forward and raised his hand dashingly in the air, exactly as they had seen Sir Hugh, through the telescope, standing on the bridge of the other ship as it cut across their path.

Captain Wrick shook his head in contempt. He had never seen a ship ignore the emergency flag before. It had passed them now and was pitching in the waves at the exit from the harbour. Captain Wrick turned the wheel, swung the *Fortune Bey* back before the wind and headed straight for the dock.

Bartlett glanced at Jacques.

'What do you think Sir Hugh Lough was doing sailing out of the harbour?' he murmured. He thought for a moment. 'You don't think the Queen lost faith in us? You don't suppose she gave up hope that we were coming back?'

Jacques raised an eyebrow.

'No, Jacques.'

Jacques cocked his head and glanced up at the sky. Bartlett knew what he was thinking. He began to calculate, trying to remember the exact date. Suddenly he understood. He gasped.

'It's seven months, isn't it?'

'To the day,' said Jacques.

Chapter 20

THE NEWS THAT Bartlett had landed whipped through the town. The courtiers flocked to the Throne-room to see the wiry fellow and his big friend appear. The Queen waited on her throne. She had just come back from the harbour, where she had sent off Sir Hugh Lough in a ship that she had bought especially for him. She looked away in embarrassment each time she met Lord Ronald's eyes, as if she were just waiting for him to say 'I told you so'. But Lord Ronald of Tull did not say 'I told you so'. He didn't need to. The Queen was saying it for him, over and over, to herself.

Eventually the Queen beckoned, and Lord Ronald went over to the throne.

'Closer, Lord Ronald,' the Queen said. 'I suppose,' she whispered, 'that we should send a fast boat to overtake Sir Hugh and bring him back.'

Lord Ronald shrugged. 'I would not be so hasty, Madam' he murmured, gazing calmly at the courtiers who were watching as he whispered with the Queen. 'It would not do Sir Hugh any great harm to spend a few weeks looking for a melidrop.'

The Queen smiled sheepishly. 'Perhaps you are right,

Lord Ronald,' she whispered. 'Perhaps I am not the only person who should learn a lesson out of this.'

Lord Ronald nodded gravely, taking four or five steps back from the throne with great solemnity. It was an unusually humble remark from the Queen and it pleased him greatly.

But there was nothing humble about Sutton Pufrock, who was just arriving at the palace, carried by four of his neighbours. Through the streets he came, waving his stick in triumph and whooping with delight from his stretcher, shouting 'That'll show Hughie Lough!' as he went round each corner. Even when he had been placed on a table in the Throne-room he continued muttering excitedly and occasionally cried out loudly enough for the Queen herself to hear a contemptuous 'Loughy *Duffy!*' coming from his direction. She had to send a footman to clasp a hand over his mouth every time his excitement got the better of him.

Eventually Bartlett arrived. The Royal Usher bashed his staff on the ground and announced him from the doorway of the Throne-room. He was flanked by Jacques le Grand and Gozo. The trio strode straight towards the throne. All around there was a hush. Only Sutton Pufrock broke the silence, triumphantly crying *'Bart—'* before being stifled by the quick hand of the footman.

They stopped in front of the Queen. The Queen

glanced at Bartlett and Jacques le Grand for a moment, then she looked carefully at Gozo.

'I do not remember *this* one,' she remarked to Lord Ronald.

'His name is Gozo,' said Bartlett.

'Indeed?' said the Queen. 'Don't tell me *he* helped you. He is rather young, don't you think?'

Gozo stared fixedly at the Queen. He was too overwhelmed by the massive palace, the magnificent Throne-room and the Queen herself to say anything. In fact, he was too overwhelmed to get excited.

'He was indispensable,' said Bartlett. 'So was his Uncle Mordi.'

'Really?' said the Queen. 'Then we thank you *and* your Uncle Mordi,' she said, nodding in Gozo's direction.

Gozo's eyes were wider than ever.

The Queen smiled. 'And we thank *you*,' she said, turning to Jacques le Grand.

Jacques nodded in return.

The Queen looked back at Bartlett. 'You *have* brought back a melidrop, I presume.'

'Yes,' said Bartlett.

'May we see it?'

'Certainly,' replied Bartlett.

Bartlett untied a small canvas bag that was hanging from his belt. The Queen watched him in surprise. This was hardly the golden casket that Sir Hugh Lough had

160

taken with him. A moment later Bartlett extracted a small fruit, no larger than a child's fist. Its colour was bright red and it had yellow streaks, and it looked as fresh as if it had been picked only that morning.

A footman stepped forward holding a fine silver tray. Bartlett placed the melidrop on the tray and the footman carried it to the Queen. The Queen peered at the fruit. She bent forward and sniffed it. She glanced at Lord Ronald with a look of extreme satisfaction, reached out her hand, and picked the melidrop up.

She dropped it at once, with a shriek.

The melidrop bounced off the footman's tray and rolled across the floor. Quick as a flash, Gozo scrambled forwards and grabbed it.

'It's hard!' the Queen cried. 'Hard as a rock. I can't eat *that!* Mr Bartlett, what sort of trick do you think you are playing? If you think this is funny, you are wrong, very wrong indeed. He is wrong, is he not, Lord Ronald?'

'It's frozen,' Bartlett replied calmly.

'What is?' demanded the Queen.

'The melidrop,' said Bartlett. 'It's still frozen. That's how we preserved it.'

'Frozen?' said the Queen. She frowned. 'How on earth did you freeze it?'

'Well, it's quite a long story. We got an iceberg.'

'An iceberg?' said the Queen. 'An iceberg?' she repeated softly, turning to Lord Ronald.

161

Lord Ronald nodded, smiling with amazement.

'I'm afraid that's why we took so long,' said Bartlett. 'Getting the iceberg took quite a while.'

'I'm sure it did,' said the Queen. She gazed at Bartlett with wonder, as if she didn't know quite what to think.

Bartlett shrugged. 'I couldn't think of any other way, you see.'

'But Mr Bartlett, I have never heard of anyone doing that before. *Should* I have heard of it?'

'I don't think so,' said Bartlett. 'I'd never heard of it either.'

The Queen continued to gaze at Bartlett. 'Well, that is most extraordinary,' she said eventually. 'Most exceptional. Most...'

'Exhilarating?'

'Yes. Thank you, Lord Ronald. It is *most* exhilarating. An iceberg? Mr Bartlett, however did you come to think of it?'

'Inventiveness!' cried Sutton Pufrock, 'Desperation and—'

'Perseverance,' said Bartlett, as Sutton Pufrock's voice was stifled by the footman. 'He's right, Your Highness, it took all of those. It took all of those and more.'

'It's hard to imagine Sir Hugh coming up with that idea,' murmured Lord Ronald, and the Queen couldn't keep herself from smiling.

'Well, that was *very* exceptional, Mr Bartlett,' she said.

'Very exhilarating.'

'Thank you.'

The Queen glanced at the melidrop sitting in Gozo's hand, as if she had only just remembered it. 'One *can* still eat this melidrop, I presume?'

'Yes,' said Bartlett.

'When?'

'You will have to wait a little.'

'Yet *more* waiting!' the Queen cried impulsively.

Lord Ronald smiled. There was, it appeared, nothing better than a melidrop to teach patience to a Queen.

'How long must I wait?' inquired the Queen.

'Not long,' said Bartlett. 'Until it thaws properly. Tomorrow, probably.'

The Queen sighed. 'Tomorrow?' she asked.

'For breakfast,' said Bartlett.

The Chief Butler took the melidrop and placed it in a beautiful silver box lined by cotton wool. He deposited it on a shelf in the pantry that was reserved for delicacies, spices and food items of exceptional rarity, where the temperature was even and cool and the melidrop could thaw at a moderate rate. Then he locked the door so that no one could get to it. But Gozo, who had not come all this way with a melidrop from Mordi's farm just to see someone come along and steal it at the last minute, announced that he was going to sit in front of the pantry door and guard it all night. And that is exactly where he was, fast asleep, when the Chief Butler, Bartlett, Jacques le Grand and the Head Chef came back to get the melidrop the next morning. The Chief Butler stepped over him, unlocked the door, got the box with the melidrop and stepped over him once again, and Gozo didn't wake up until they had taken the melidrop out of the box and were all standing around the table in the middle of the Queen's great kitchen, examining it.

The melidrop's skin looked almost perfect. It still had the wrinkles that were there when Mordi first discovered it. Bartlett turned it over and everyone scrutinised the other side. A slight bruise had appeared near one end, which must have occurred the previous day when the Queen threw the melidrop back at the footman and it bounced on the floor.

Bartlett picked the melidrop up. He squeezed it tentatively. He sniffed it. The Head Chef watched him, waiting. Bartlett gave the melidrop to Jacques and then to Gozo. They tested it gently as well. The melidrop had thawed but was still firm. It had a sweet but fresh aroma.

Bartlett looked at Gozo. Gozo nodded. Jacques nodded as well.

'It's ready,' Bartlett said, and he handed the melidrop to the Head Chef.

The Head Chef took his sharpest knife and cleanly split the melidrop in two. He placed the halves face up

on a plate of the finest white porcelain.

The yellow flesh of the melidrop glistened invitingly. Suddenly Jacques remembered the delicious sweetness of the melidrops that he had eaten in the bazaar, and it was all he could do to stop himself leaping at the fruit and wolfing it down in two bites. The Head Chef put the plate on a bright silver tray together with a delicate silver spoon. He gave the tray to the Chief Butler. The Chief Butler carried the tray out. Bartlett, Jacques le Grand and Gozo followed.

The Queen was already waiting in her breakfast room. A crowd of courtiers had gathered to watch her eat the melidrop. The crisp white tablecloth was entirely bare except for a glass and a crystal jug of pure mountain water. The Chief Butler placed the melidrop in front of the Queen. The Queen picked up the silver spoon. She looked at the cut melidrop for a moment. Then she took a small scoop of the melidrop's flesh and placed it daintily in her mouth.

The Queen chewed slowly. Her face remained completely expressionless. She swallowed. She put her spoon back into the melidrop and took another scoop.

The Queen ate the whole melidrop without saying a word. Her expression did not change. She cleaned out one half of the melidrop, took a sip of water, and then cleaned out the other half. No one could tell what she was thinking.

When she had finished the Queen took another sip from her glass of pure mountain water. Then she sat back in her chair. She gazed at the plate in front of her for a long time. The two empty halves of the red melidrop stared back at her, hollowed-out pieces of skin with yellow streaks that would soon start to curl and darken and wither away.

Finally she looked up. 'I believe we had a deal, Mr Bartlett.'

'Yes,' said Bartlett.

'I said that I would provide an expedition if you brought me a melidrop before I sent Sir Hugh. And you said that you would be back within seven months. So I'm afraid you did not fulfil your side of the bargain. You arrived three hours after the seven months were up, and Sir Hugh had already been sent.'

Bartlett didn't reply. He glanced at Jacques. Jacques gave a faint shrug. He didn't really expect anything better from the Queen.

Suddenly the Queen smiled. 'But I *will* provide your expedition,' she said, speaking directly to Jacques le Grand, whose shrug she had seen. She turned to Bartlett. 'It will give me great pleasure to provide it. I have never heard of anything so clever or so ... desperate, or even so inventive, as getting an iceberg. I have never heard of anything that even comes close to it. I admit, I doubted your dedication, Bartlett. You have proved me wrong.'

There was a stifled gasp from the courtiers. They tried to remember when they had last heard the Queen admit a mistake.

'Oh, yes,' said the Queen, looking around. 'I was wrong. And there is another lesson I have learned,' she said, glancing at Lord Ronald, 'the importance of patience. And trust, that is also important, when there is one who is worthy of it.'

The courtiers stared at her in amazement.

'Why are you so surprised?' said the Queen, 'I have always been eager to learn from experience.'

The courtiers shuffled nervously. Something very strange had happened to the Queen since Bartlett had come back with the melidrop. They even wondered whether she had been writing poems again.

Bartlett nodded. 'I have learned something also, Madam. I did not think that going to get a melidrop could be a real adventure. But it was. It was one of the greatest adventures of my life.'

Jacques le Grand raised an eyebrow. Bartlett was going a bit too far!

'Now, tell me something else, Mr Bartlett,' said the Queen. 'Could you have brought back more than one melidrop? Two perhaps, or three? Or a dozen?'

'Probably,' said Bartlett. 'But you only asked for one.'

The Queen laughed. 'So I did! I only asked for one.' Suddenly she gazed at the melidrop skins on the plate in front of her. After a moment she sighed. 'Well,' she murmured, speaking to no one in particular, 'I suppose it wouldn't have mattered if there *were* a few more. Eventually they would have gone as well.'

A faint, thoughtful smile came across the Queen's lips. 'Perhaps, after all, it is not such a good idea to ask for things like melidrops. I suspect that as soon as you have had the last one, you will always want another.'

If you have enjoyed this title, why not try something else by Bloomsbury ...

HARRY POTTER

and the Philosopher's Stone

J.K. ROWLING

9¾

GOLD AWARD WINNER
1997
AGES 9-11
Smarties
Book Prize

HOGWARTS EXPRESS

"...this is a terrific book." *The Sunday Telegraph*

J.K.ROWLING

HARRY POTTER

and the Chamber of Secrets

'Splendiferous and delightful' *The Sunday Times*

HARRY POTTER

POTTER

and the Prisoner of Azkaban

J.K.ROWLING

DOUBLE SMARTIES AWARD-WINNING AUTHOR

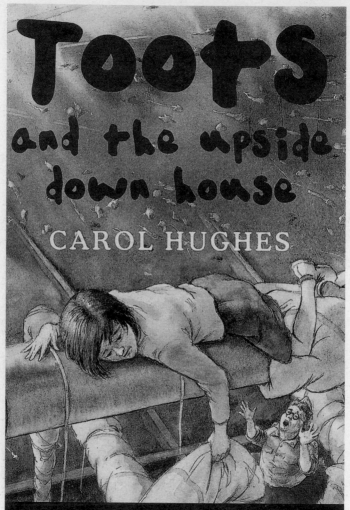

Toots
and the upside down house

CAROL HUGHES

'Toots has the makings of a modern classic' *Sandi Toksvig*

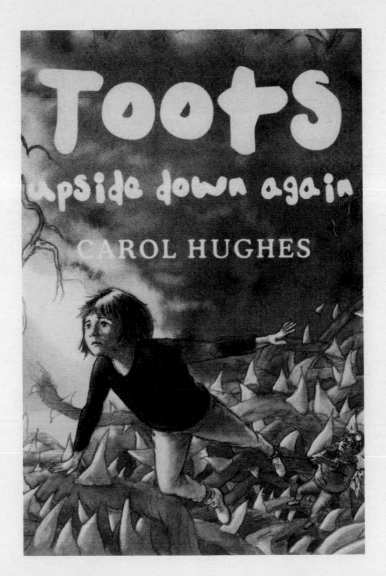

Toots
underwater

CAROL HUGHES

'Toots has the makings of a modern classic' *Sandi Toksvig*